Sierra paused next to him. "I didn't mean to impose."

"You didn't," Dallas answered levelly. He'd have to agree to something for it to be an imposition.

"Still..." She looked contrite.

"Don't worry about it." He stepped aside, both to let her pass and to put some distance between them. The sexual buzz was unsettling. And the very last thing he wanted to do was figure out if she felt it too.

"I will appreciate any help," she said. "I mean, maybe not tomorrow."

"Maybe not from me," he responded, wanting to shut the notion down right from the start. He wasn't about to indulge his unwelcome attraction.

Silence rested between them for a few seconds.

Then she canted her head and gave a smile that amped his awareness up even further. "You're a tough nut to crack."

"I won't crack." He wouldn't—not on either front.

* * *

Breakaway Cowboy by Barbara Dunlop
is part of the High Country Hawkes series.

Dear Reader,

Welcome to book one of the High Country Hawkes series, *Breakaway Cowboy*. This new series is a return to my roots of ranching, cowboys and the wide-open range.

The Hawkes family has ranched the Colorado high country for seven generations, and current patriarch Garrett Hawkes is determined that his sons and daughter continue the family legacy.

In *Breakaway Cowboy*, middle son Dallas reluctantly returns home after ten years on the rodeo circuit to heal from a career-ending shoulder injury. Once there, he's forced to face painful memories of his mother's death. Following a betrayal and breakup with her fiancé, California wellness coach Sierra Armstrong is recruited by her college friend McKinney Hawkes to go undercover as a ranch hand trainee and secretly help Dallas cope with his frustration.

Her ineptitude on the ranch has Sierra running afoul of the aloof and ruggedly sexy Dallas as she tries to get close enough to help him. Dallas struggles to keep his distance from the intriguing, tenacious Sierra. But when she asks for his help and instruction, he can't stop himself from engaging, amping up the fiery attraction between them.

I hope you enjoy the story!

Barbara

BARBARA DUNLOP

BREAKAWAY COWBOY

ISBN-13: 978-1-335-58169-3

Breakaway Cowboy

Copyright © 2023 by Barbara Dunlop

For questions and comments about the quality of this book, please contact us at CustomerService@Harlequin.com.

Harlequin Enterprises ULC
22 Adelaide St. West, 41st Floor
Toronto, Ontario M5H 4E3, Canada
www.Harlequin.com

Printed in U.S.A.

New York Times and *USA TODAY* bestselling author **Barbara Dunlop** has written more than fifty novels for Harlequin, including the acclaimed Gambling Men series for Harlequin Desire. Her flirty, lighthearted stories regularly hit bestseller lists, with one of her novels made into a TV movie. Barbara is a four-time finalist for the Romance Writers of America's RITA® Award.

Books by Barbara Dunlop

Harlequin Desire

Gambling Men

The Twin Switch
The Dating Dare
Midnight Son
Husband in Name Only

High Country Hawkes

Breakaway Cowboy

Visit the Author Profile page
at Harlequin.com for more titles.

You can also find Barbara Dunlop on Facebook, along with other Harlequin Desire authors, at Facebook.com/HarlequinDesireAuthors!

One

Dallas Hawkes paced his way through the bone-dry horse corral at the Hawkes Cattle Ranch in northwestern Colorado, his boots stirring a mini dust cloud with every step. He flinched at the pain that shot through his right shoulder, more impatient with the injury now than in the three weeks since he'd returned home.

Jaw clenched, he cussed silently so he wouldn't spook his roan gelding, Jayden, standing by the fence tacked up and ready to go. Jayden's dark eyes showed mild curiosity at Dallas's steady approach. Without breaking stride, Dallas unsnapped the pocket of his denim shirt, popped the top of his prescription bottle and tossed a tablet to the back of his throat, swallowing hard.

He'd prefer two tablets, the dose he'd taken last week. But he wasn't falling into that trap. One pill four times a day now, and he was determined to cut back even further starting Monday.

He patted Jayden firmly on the shoulder. Then he raised his tanned face to the noonday summer sun, resetting his Stetson and drawing a deep bracing breath.

He'd fought through injuries many times before. And this wasn't that much worse. It only felt worse because it was happening right now. A couple of more weeks, maybe a month, and the sharp pain would fade to sore, then to an irritant. Soon it would be nothing but a memory, just like all his other breaks, dislocations and soft-tissue tears.

He gathered the reins and steeled himself for the mount. No matter how much it hurt, he was determined to get up on horseback today. A man needed hard work to focus his mind.

He missed riding, missed the motivation and power of the animal beneath him, missed the bond that came from their wordless communication. But what he missed most of all was the thrill and action of the rodeo circuit.

The other guys would be in Tulsa by now, calf roping or steer wrestling. He doubted the bareback riding would have started this early in the day. Maybe mutton busting. Despite his frustration, he couldn't help but smile as he thought of the little cowpokes riding frisky sheep, beaming and so proud of themselves if they managed to stay on until the buzzer.

Jayden shifted his feet, reminding Dallas that he was putting off the inevitable.

"You coming or what?" Dallas's older brother, Austin, called out from beside the barn.

"On my way," Dallas returned, bracing his hand on the saddle horn and stuffing his boot into the stirrup. He took most of his weight on his leg and swung his hips over the horse's back, cringing and sucking in a tight breath as he settled deep into the saddle.

Man, that had hurt.

Luckily, Jayden was patient with Dallas's awkward mount.

Laying the reins across his palm, he urged the horse into a walk, feeling every step and hoping the painkiller kicked in soon.

"You sure you're up for this?" Austin asked as Dallas approached, his brow furrowed under his tan Stetson.

"You my nursemaid now?" Dallas asked gruffly in return, resenting his brother for fussing.

"It's an hour to the pump station."

"I know how far we're going."

"It's been a while since you've been out on the range." Austin turned his black-spotted stallion, Pepper, to pick up a walk next to Jayden.

Dallas heard a judgmental edge to his brother's tone and told himself to ignore it. His mood was testy enough already.

He kept his own voice carefully even but felt honor bound to respond. "I haven't been gone that long."

Austin gave a chopped dry laugh. "The better part of a decade."

"I've contributed more than just time and labor." Competing on the rodeo circuit kept Dallas out of Colorado most of the year. But hitting all the events was the best way to maximize his winnings. They'd been consistent, and he'd sent most of the money home to support the family ranch.

He didn't need much on the road—diesel fuel, discount motels, fast food and the occasional bottle of bourbon.

He flexed his shoulder now, thinking a shot of bourbon would probably kickstart the painkiller.

"Nobody said you hadn't," Austin said.

"Right," Dallas drawled.

"You're paranoid. I saw the checks you sent. Nobody's complaining."

Dallas was surprised to hear Austin had seen the checks. He'd sent them directly to his father, Garrett, and hadn't expected anyone else in the family to know the details of his contributions.

Austin kept talking. "All I'm saying is that it's been a while since you've been here, boots on the ground."

"They're on the ground now," Dallas responded. He wished they weren't but wishing alone didn't make anything come true.

"And it's good that you're back."

Dallas snorted sharply in response, then immediately regretted it when Jayden danced beneath him, jarring his shoulder once more.

"You might not want to be here." Austin's tone was unsympathetic. "But here is where you are. It is what it is, little brother."

"At least it put Dad in a good mood." Dallas steered the conversation away from his own situation.

His father had been pushing him for years to give up the rodeo life and settle down on the ranch. Dallas, on the other hand, got twitchy just thinking about nothing but these two valleys year in, year out.

"It's not all about Dad."

Dallas begged to disagree. "When has it *not* been all about him?"

Austin peered from beneath his hat brim. "You really do need a change of attitude."

"What I need—" Dallas stopped himself. What he needed was for his shoulder to heal so he could get back out on the circuit. Or if not the rodeo circuit, then at least somewhere different, somewhere new, somewhere that wasn't...here, to be precise, where memories crowded in and he felt like he was going backward in time.

A shrill whistle sounded, and both horses lifted their heads, their ears pointing forward.

Up on the rise, Hardy Rawlings waved his hat as he galloped toward them.

Austin kicked Pepper into a trot to meet the longtime ranch hand.

Dallas reflexively lifted his heels to hurry Jayden, stopping himself just in time.

"Sections of the Golden Ridge cross fence came down in the wind," Hardy called out as he grew closer. He slid his horse to a halt on the stiff grass in front of Austin, and the gelding pranced in place. "Halfway across the meadow below Signal Peak."

Austin turned Pepper in a tight circle to keep the horse from reacting to Hardy's agitated mount. "Is it bad?"

"Bad enough. A bunch of the central herd crossed over. They're scattered along the creek all the way up to Woody Springs."

"Great," Austin snapped, obviously worried about water management through such a dry summer.

"Willis rode down to the cookhouse to get more hands," Hardy said as Dallas came up beside them.

"I'll head out with you now." Austin looked to Dallas. "You be okay?"

Dallas frowned. He couldn't keep the sarcasm out of his voice this time. "You mean when I'm left behind like a child?"

Austin's jaw tensed and his brow shot up. "You saying you want to ride out with us?"

Dallas definitely wanted to ride out with them. He badly wanted to ride out to the range and roust the errant cattle from the bushes and hollows, then herd them back to where they belonged.

The painkiller had started kicking in, giving him confidence.

"Yeah," he said.

Hardy shot him a questioning look.

There was a beat of silence before Austin answered with a dispassionate shrug. "Suit yourself." Then he turned his horse while Hardy turned his, and the two men raced up the rise.

Dallas kicked Jayden into a trot behind them, which was excruciating on his shoulder. He urged the horse into a gallop instead, which was smoother and slightly less painful. He knew he was going to pay a price for this later. But, for now, the ripple of muscle beneath his body and the controlled power under his hands and heels felt intoxicatingly familiar.

Forget how he'd feel tonight or tomorrow. For this moment, he was back.

Sierra Armstrong tugged hard on her engagement ring, hating that her finger was swelling in the hot July humidity of Carmel, California. She stood face-to-face with her fiancé—correction, her *ex*-fiancé—on the city sidewalk in front of Opuntia Lifestyles. They were three blocks from the beach, so tourists and residents streamed past between the shops and galleries along the strip on a Friday afternoon.

She grimaced. "I might just have to keep it."

Roger's tone turned impatient. "Sierra."

"Don't *Sierra* me." She continued tugging on the ring, even though her knuckle hurt and was starting to turn pink and puffy. She suspected she was only making things worse. "This ring was a promise. You broke your promise when you cheated on me."

"You know I didn't mean for that to happen."

Her anger peaked. "So, it was an accident? Like, oops, you tripped and fell into your receptionist's bed?"

Roger clamped his jaw.

She wasn't proud of the outburst. And she wasn't proud of her next thought either—wondering how much she might get for the diamond. The stone wasn't huge, but it wasn't tiny either.

Then she gave up with a huff. "It's not coming off."

"Let me—" Roger reached for her left hand.

She snatched it out of his reach. There wasn't a single chance she was letting him touch her ever again.

She took a step back to put more distance between them. "I'll get it off later." She'd have more success after the sun went down and the air released some of its oppressive humidity.

Roger's nostrils flared, and she could see the suspicion on his face.

Good. Let him worry she might keep the ring. She was technically entitled to it—the legal category of a gift and all that.

"Drop it by the condo later," he said.

The statement was both an order and an assertion of ownership.

She stiffened her spine against the order. But, to be completely fair, Roger did own the condo. Sierra had only moved in three months ago when her former roommate and dear friend Nancy Wells took a new job in LA. Roger's name was on the lease. Plus, the rent was paid by Opuntia Lifestyles, the company he owned and where she worked.

In the space of fifteen minutes, Sierra was single, unemployed and homeless.

She hoisted her tote bag higher on her shoulder, unsure of what to do next. Part of her wanted to storm away and never come back. Another part wanted to march straight to the condo and commandeer whatever was hers.

"I'll be home by ten, then," he stated flatly. "We're going out to—"

"We?" Sierra faltered on the word. "You mean you and Diva?"

"Devin," he corrected.

Sierra couldn't help picturing the perky new receptionist with her rosy cheeks, multicolored eye shadow and that fashion-forward winged liner. The brilliance of her bright smile had had Sierra considering a dental appointment for whitening.

"You're suggesting I conveniently drop off my engagement ring *after* your date?" She couldn't believe his audacity.

"You don't have to be so—"

"Oh, yes I do." Her hands curled up at her sides. "You should leave, Roger."

He glanced perplexedly at the sign to his business.

He was right.

She was the one who should leave.

She turned on her heel then, striding away, heading… She didn't know where she was heading. But she did know she wouldn't *drop by later* like a good little ex to hand over the custom-designed engagement ring.

Maybe she'd never go back. Maybe she'd mail the ring to him instead: parcel post. Let him wait a few weeks to get it.

Then again, her clothes were at Roger's, her toiletries too. She hadn't moved in with much, selling her bed and dining table and sending her few linens and dishes to LA with Nancy. But what she did own she wanted back, like the pair of pretty wineglasses she'd bought at a local glass blowing shop.

On the other hand, they'd used those glasses to toast their engagement. Did she really want to keep them?

Most of her lotion bottles and makeup tubes were less than half full. Her clothes were inexpensive and well-worn. She'd arrived with an attractive set of ceramic pots that were growing some healthy succulents in the bay window. But the succulents would be cumbersome to move. And the pots hadn't been all that expensive in the first place.

As she marched down the road toward the beach, she cataloged her worldly possessions residing at Roger's.

The collection might be a little thin, but right now she was glad of that.

Her truly important treasures were in a safe-deposit box at City Center Bank.

She crossed at the traffic light, paced along the sidewalk and onto the strip of lawn that ran between the road and beach. There she kicked off her sandals and stepped onto the sand.

She turned to walk under the dappled shade of the cypress trees that lined the shore. The warm sand was soothing. Its natural reflexology and exfoliation helped calm her down.

Her phone jangled and vibrated against the small of her back. She slung the roomy tote bag around to her front and pulled it open to peer inside.

She didn't want to talk to anyone right now. But new appointments might have been booked for this afternoon. It wasn't fair to leave any of her clients hanging.

Or were they Roger's clients now? Contractually, they were clients of Opuntia Lifestyles. As a licensed practitioner, she offered mind-body wellness coaching and massage therapy, helping people examine and improve their lives and better understand the connection between their emotional and physical health.

As she rooted through her bag she thought about the future for her professional practice. She'd signed a noncompete clause when she started at Opuntia. At the time, she hadn't imagined ever leaving on not-great terms.

Bad decision that.

This was her year for bad decisions.

She found her phone and checked the screen.

Her heart lifted when she saw the name McKinney Hawkes. She hadn't heard from her college friend in months. But here was McKinney, just when Sierra needed her.

She took the call. "McKinney," she said on a breathless sigh and angled across a bike path to a nearby park bench, dropping to sit down. "How did you know?"

"I don't know what it is I know." McKinney jumped in on a laugh as if no time had passed since they last talked. "But I'm sure all ears to hear about it."

"That I needed a friend." Sierra set her sandals and tote bag on the bench and leaned back to stretch her bare feet out in front of her.

McKinney's tone immediately sobered. "Why? What's wrong? What's going on?"

"Everything. Everything's wrong." Sierra couldn't hold back the catch in her voice.

"Whoa, whoa. Start at the beginning."

Sierra blinked against a sudden sting at the back of her eyes.

"Are you sick?" McKinney asked into the short silence. "Is it serious?"

"No." Sierra shook her head. "I'm not sick. It's nothing like that."

On the other end of the call, McKinney blew out a sigh of relief. "Thank goodness."

"It's Roger."

"Your boyfriend, right? I should have guessed."

Sierra felt a fresh wave of loss as a young couple rode past side by side, a sleeping toddler nestled in the child's seat on the man's bike.

"He was my fiancé," Sierra admitted. "*Was* being the operative word."

"You're engaged? I mean, you two split? Wait, what did that man do?"

The quick accusation coaxed a smile from Sierra. Like a good friend would, McKinney assumed Sierra had been wronged.

"He cheated," Sierra said on a bitter note, her eyes drying as she made the decision to stop with the self-pity. She would *not* miss a man who'd so thoroughly disappointed her.

"Big mistake," McKinney said staunchly. "Huge mistake. What was he even *thinking*? He didn't deserve you in the first place—obviously. He's never going to do better. The fool."

"Thank you."

"There's nothing to thank me for. I'm only stating the truth."

"You've never even met him."

"I don't have to meet him to know he didn't deserve you. Who cheats on their fiancée? A prize jerk, that's who. I hope you kept the ring."

Sierra glanced at her still-swollen finger. "He asked for it back. But I can't seem to get it off my finger."

"Well, that's karma for you." McKinney paused. "Is it big? Worth anything?"

"It's not like I'm going to pawn it."

"Do it," McKinney urged. "Send him the pawn ticket if you feel guilty. If he wants it back, he can buy it from Bruno or Snake."

Despite herself, Sierra's smile widened. "Bruno or Snake?"

"Pawnshop owners have great nicknames." McKinney sounded feisty and fearless, just like she'd been all through college. "And they charge a hefty markup. They're good guys when you need them on your side."

"People don't much mess with you, do they?"

"How do you think I survived three older brothers?"

"You told me your brothers were wonderful."

"They are. Now. They weren't always."

"You're lucky." Sierra couldn't keep the catch from her voice, suddenly feeling both envious and lonely.

She had no sisters or brothers. And when her mother died five years ago, her father had already moved to Florida with his new wife and family.

"I'm coming to California," McKinney stated with conviction.

The pledge startled Sierra. "What?"

"You need me. For moral support if nothing else. I can be on a plane tomorrow."

"No. No. You can't disrupt your life." Sierra wasn't about to let McKinney get dragged down in this drama.

As the sun made its way toward the Pacific, her thoughts turned to where she would sleep tonight. An inexpensive motel seemed like the most reasonable option, something with a kitchenette so she didn't have to eat in restaurants. She had some savings, but being out of a job, she couldn't afford to throw her money around.

"Sure, I can," McKinney insisted. "There are plenty of direct flights from Denver to California."

"No."

"Yes."

"McKinney."

"What?"

"I don't have…a place to live right now. I can't put you up if you come to Carmel."

McKinney was silent for a beat. "He made *you* be the one to move out?"

"It's his condo."

"I don't care."

"It's his business too, Opuntia Lifestyles." The feeling of hopelessness rushed back, overwhelming Sierra. The sinking sun seemed to mock her predicament. "Everything is his."

"Whoa. What? See, this is why I needed you to start from the beginning. I thought you two were colleagues."

Sierra had glossed over their business relationship. "I wasn't all that comfortable at first. You know, dating the boss."

There was another moment of silence before McKinney spoke. "Come here."

Sierra didn't understand.

"Come to Jagged Creek," McKinney continued. "It's the easiest thing in the world. You fly into Denver. There's a bus every hour to Granby. I can meet you at the junction. Just text me your details."

Sierra was deeply touched by the offer. But she wasn't about to impose on McKinney, never mind on her family at their ranch.

Sierra needed to put her life back together. She needed to find a new job and a new place to live, not to go traipsing halfway across the country to hide out from her problems—even if it did sound tempting.

"I can't come to Jagged Creek," she said.

"Sure, you can. I just told you how."

"That's not what I—"

"And, anyway, that's the reason why I called in the first place." McKinney's tone changed, going deeper, more serious. "I need your help, Sierra."

It was Sierra's turn to be alarmed. "Why? What's wrong?"

"It's my brother Dallas, the middle one. He got hurt rodeoing."

"Oh, no." Sierra felt incredibly selfish for letting the whole conversation be about her.

"He took a bad fall bronc riding," McKinney said.

Sierra's stomach sank. "How bad?"

"He'll heal. Well, mostly, at least physically. But his rodeo career is likely over. And he's angry about that. He's angry about most everything right now. And he gets more withdrawn by the day. Sierra. I don't know how to help him."

Sierra's professionalism immediately kicked in. "What's he doing, saying?"

"Anything sets him off. *Everything* sets him off."

"I'd be happy to do a session with him." These days, Sierra worked with several remote clients.

"No. No. He definitely won't go for that. He's not a… you know…self-helpy kind of guy. We can't tell him who you are or what you do. He'll clam up for sure."

Sierra had to be honest. "I don't see how I can help him, then." If a client wouldn't open up, if they weren't ready to look dispassionately at their life, identify the pitfalls and start making some changes, no wellness coach in the world could help them.

"Just talk to him. Come to the ranch and talk to him, you know, casually. We'll make up a story, tell him you're a new ranch hand or something."

"A ranch hand?" Sierra didn't know a thing about ranching. She didn't have the first clue about animals. Well, dogs, maybe. She'd always loved dogs. But dogs weren't livestock. She had zero experience with cows or horses or even chickens.

"You wouldn't have to do heavy hard work. Maybe fork a little hay, sweep a few stalls, pick some vegetables. Please, Sierra. I'm scared for my family."

The plea in McKinney's voice hit Sierra straight in the heart. What wouldn't she give to have a close family? And if she did, what wouldn't she do to protect them?

"It's the perfect answer," McKinney added on a hopeful note. "It'll give you some time to think, some time to heal. We'll visit. We'll talk. We'll drink wine and diss your jerk of an ex. It'll be good for you, and it'll help me so much."

Sierra couldn't resist the entreaty in her dear friend's voice.

"Okay," she said as the sun closed in on the blue water and the pale pink horizon. "Okay, I'll come."

Two

Dallas braced the heel of his hand against the marble wall of his shower and let the hot spray pound down on his sore shoulder. The pressure hurt, but then everything had hurt today, including breathing. And he knew the heat would help with blood circulation—key to healing a soft-tissue injury.

It wasn't like he'd even worked that hard today. He'd rolled out of bed at his usual time this morning but hadn't gotten up on horseback. Instead, he'd made himself useful by driving a pickup to the valley bottom hay fields to check the irrigation system, log the growth of the graze and confirm the moisture content of the soil.

Austin was talking about automating the moisture checks, using sensors and a solar-powered satellite linkup. It sounded like they could do it all from the comfort of the home office. What kind of a cowboy wanted to stay inside all day long with his butt spreading out in a chair?

Besides, too many things could go wrong with technology. On a ranch, nothing beat ground-truthing the conditions, whether it was the crops or the animals. A rancher needed eyes on and hands on to be certain.

Having warmed his muscles and washed off the day's dirt, Dallas stepped dripping onto the woven mat outside the oversize glass cubicle of his en suite bathroom. He pulled a thick fresh towel from the shelf, awkwardly rubbing down his short hair before one-handing his way along the rest of his body, telling himself tomorrow would be better. Healing took time, and he had to find a way to be patient.

It was coming up on seven. Dinner would be served soon for the family and likely a few others. Dallas's father, Garrett, saw meals as opportunities for informal ranch meetings. Aside from the filling and delicious food, it was interesting to find out who was on the hot seat or had received Garrett's favor on any given night.

In his high-ceilinged, wooden-beamed bedroom on the second floor of the ranch house, Dallas pulled up a clean pair of jeans. Then he cautiously pushed his right arm into the sleeve of a dark green cotton shirt, snapping it up and rolling the cuffs to his elbows.

By the time he finished dressing, his dark hair was partially dry. He ran a comb through its length, full on top and short at the sides. His stubble beard could use a trim. But it was an awkward process with his left hand that could wait until tomorrow. Right now, he was starving, and the enticing aroma of slow-roasting prime rib was wafting its way up the main staircase.

The wide, curving stairs led down to the woodsy great room, richly decorated in brown leather and pale tweed with burgundy accents. It was separated from the formal dining room by six polished log pillars that matched the ceiling beams and hardwood floor. The rock fireplace was cold this time of year. Even up here in the mountains, the heat of the day kept the nighttime temperature in the midsixties. Windows were open along the dining room wall, their wine-colored curtains drawn wide to let in the fresh air.

The rectangular cherrywood table was set for six at the near end, but nobody was seated for dinner yet. His stomach growing insistent, Dallas hoped the others wouldn't take too long to arrive.

"That pretty much covers it." Dallas's sister McKinney's cheerful voice sounded in the hallway that led to the south wing of the house with its library, entertainment hall and wine cellar.

Dallas was glad to know McKinney, at least, was on her way to dinner.

"For this floor, anyway," she continued. "I'll show you around the upstairs later on. It's smaller."

"I can sure see I'm not in Kansas anymore." The voice that answered was female, mellow and easy, like a breeze through the early summer leaves. She sure didn't sound like she was from Kansas.

"It's super simple once you get the hang of it," McKinney said.

"I hope so. Man, that is one elaborate wine tasting bar."

Dallas could tell where they were standing, and he hoped they wouldn't dawdle there admiring the horseshoe-shaped bar with its eight wood-and-leather armchairs. He wanted them to get a move on to the dining room.

McKinney chuckled. "It's a thing for my dad, and his dad and maybe Great-Grandpa too. I'm not sure. They've collected for years and years. Dad still buys way too many bottles, limited editions, futures. Then he makes quite the ceremony of opening the more interesting ones."

"Not to be critical of your family," the other woman said.

"Criticize away," McKinney responded breezily. "We can take it."

Dallas's stomach protested once more. He told it to pipe down, because he liked listening to the woman's voice, and he was curious to hear what she was about to say.

"That seems a bit pretentious."

Dallas didn't disagree with that.

"He's not," McKinney said. "I mean…well…only about wine. Beyond wine, he's all rancher. A hardworking one. Serious, maybe exacting. But fair-minded, always fair-minded."

Dallas pulled a frown at McKinney's rose-colored-glasses interpretation. He'd dispute the fair-minded part, for sure. But he wasn't surprised to hear her defend their father. She always had been his favorite.

Dallas shifted to the head of the hallway where he could see the two women.

"You're lucky to have such a great family," the stranger said, sounding sincere.

He might not know what state she'd come from, but she was sure easy on the eyes.

Her long honey-blond hair was feathered around her face, while her wide startlingly blue eyes were surrounded by thick lashes and topped with impeccably sculpted brows. Her full, soft lips made a man think about kissing at midnight.

Dressed in black jeans, heeled brown ankle boots and a clingy maroon sweater, she was maybe five feet four. Her hips were slender, her breasts full, with an hourglass waist in between.

"Dallas." McKinney spotted him and sounded unusually happy about it.

The other woman met his gaze, sending an odd warmth

through him. For a moment his pain faded a notch, and he flexed his shoulder to test the odd sensation.

"This is Sierra Armstrong." McKinney started his way and Sierra Armstrong followed along. "She's a new ranch hand. Part of our equal opportunity initiative. You remember."

He didn't remember any such thing. And this Sierra was clearly the furthest thing from a ranch hand.

"Hello, Dallas," Sierra said in that same mellow tone. She flashed a dazzling smile, distracting him as she offered a slim hand.

He glanced to McKinney for an explanation. There wasn't a chance that this woman could handle ranch work.

McKinney's lips flattened with displeasure, and she looked pointedly at Sierra's waiting hand.

Acknowledging his rudeness, Dallas reached out to shake.

The minute their hands came together his focus narrowed. Hers was swallowed by his, but not in a bad way. It nestled snugly to his palm. It was smooth and cool but sent another curious warmth through his skin, over his wrist and deep into the sinew of his forearm.

"Nice to meet you," he managed before quickly letting her go. He knew sexual attraction when he felt it, and that was nothing but bad news in this instance.

"I thought you could show her the ropes tomorrow," McKinney interjected like she thought he might agree. Then she turned to Sierra. "Dallas knows the ranch as well as anyone."

"Not according to Austin." Dallas lined several convenient excuses up inside his head. No way was he getting co-opted into an equal opportunity ranch orientation with someone so unsuitable.

"I'm excited to get started," Sierra said with another disarming smile.

"I'm busy." He'd keep it vague unless McKinney pressed. "But there are plenty of experienced hands to show you around." With a perfunctory nod, he turned away to end the conversation.

His father and Austin were coming down the stairs, talking together in low tones. At the same time, ranch foreman Newt Candor emerged from the kitchen passageway.

Dallas wondered if Newt was being rewarded or in trouble for some reason. Rewarded, he hoped. It would make dinner a whole lot more pleasant.

Newt had dressed respectfully. His gray slacks and dress shirt were pressed and clean. His hair was freshly washed, but there was no hiding his calloused hands and fifty-something weathered face. Those were all working cowhand.

"Hey, Newt," Dallas greeted the man with a nod. He liked Newt, and he was glad dinner was finally getting underway.

"You can't be that busy," McKinney said from behind him, impatience in her tone.

"How're you holding up?" Newt asked Dallas. Then he spotted Garrett on the stairs and gave the boss a nod of acknowledgment. "Mr. Hawkes."

"Evening, Newt," Dallas's father replied as he came to the bottom. His tone was even, telling Dallas nothing about his mood or Newt's potential fate.

"Dallas?" McKinney prompted in a sharper tone.

Everyone looked her way.

Dallas had no choice but to acknowledge her question. He turned and raised an impatient brow.

"So, tomorrow?" she asked.

"I told you, I'm busy tomorrow." Someone else could jump in and babysit McKinney's pet project.

Dallas was keeping himself focused on the minute-to-minute work while he was stuck here on the ranch. It didn't pay to get distracted or let his mind wander. Plus, the very last thing he needed was a glamorous audience while he struggled awkwardly through his day.

McKinney cocked her head. "With what?"

Sierra spoke up. "McKinney, there's no need to push—"

The cook, Victor Russell, burst into the dining room, attracting everyone's attention to the sizzling roast he carried on a large platter. He paused abruptly and looked to Garrett, clearly wondering if he'd jumped the gun on serving dinner.

"Let's all sit down," Dallas's father said, moving to the head of the table.

McKinney spoke in an undertone as she passed Dallas. "We'll talk later."

He shook his head to tell her they wouldn't, at least not about this. But she'd already moved on.

Sierra paused next to him. "I didn't mean to impose."

"You didn't," he answered levelly. He'd have to agree to something for it to be an imposition.

"Still…" She looked contrite.

"Don't worry about it." He stepped aside, both to let her pass and to put some distance between them. The sexual buzz was unsettling. And the very last thing he wanted to do was figure out if she felt it too.

Instead of moving, she spoke again. "McKinney is very enthusiastic."

"I got that."

In the dining room, chairs scraped against the floor and muted voices sounded as the others took their places at the table. The prime rib was a strong pull, but Dallas wasn't about to rudely leave Sierra standing here.

"I will appreciate any help," she said. "I mean, maybe not tomorrow."

"Maybe not from me," he responded, wanting to shut the notion down right from the start. He wasn't about to indulge his unwelcome attraction.

Silence rested between them for a few seconds.

Then she canted her head and gave a philosophical smile that amped his awareness up even further. "You're a tough nut to crack."

"I won't crack." He wouldn't—not on either front.

Sierra was awed by the opulence of her assigned bedroom and gratified by the comfort of the king-size bed. She hadn't expected to sleep well last night, but she'd dropped off in seconds and slept soundly. That was all before she even discovered the two-nozzle shower in the massive bathroom with its separate deep soaker tub and arched window overlooking the valley. She'd known McKinney's family owned a vast Colorado ranch, but she sure hadn't expected to stay in a mansion.

The faded blue jeans, checked flannel shirt and scuffed leather boots she'd borrowed from McKinney looked out of place in the lavish surroundings. But McKinney had insisted the well-worn outfit was the right choice for her disguise, dismissing the casual clothes Sierra had picked up before her flight yesterday as too trendy.

Even if she didn't wear them right away, the shopping trip had felt liberating to Sierra, an important part of leaving her old life completely behind.

Buying new clothes had also left her feeling unmoored. But that was to be expected. And her training would help her through the turmoil.

Change was complicated. It was often difficult. And she knew she was making change upon change upon change right now. Luckily, she knew to roll with it and take things one day at a time.

For the moment, she had a place to stay and a purpose for being here. Her long-term decisions could come later, after her mind had grown accustomed to the abrupt turn of events.

She twisted her hair into a neat French braid to embrace the day. She couldn't bring herself to completely skip her makeup, but she settled for a light foundation with sunscreen, some mascara and a natural shade of lipstick.

She couldn't carry a purse while working in the barn. Then again, she couldn't imagine why she'd need cash or credit cards out here. So, she tucked her phone in her back pocket and left everything else in her room.

She took the secondary staircase she and McKinney had used last night. Then, on the main floor, she got turned around in the hallways. But eventually she came out at the wine bar and oriented herself.

"That's not equal opportunity." Dallas sounded annoyed in the distance as she approached the great room. "That's preferential treatment."

"Are you suggesting the bunkhouse?" McKinney asked with an edge of sarcasm.

"She can sleep in the staff quarters in the south wing," Dallas answered back.

Sierra stopped as she realized they were talking about her. But it was too late. She was in the great room now, and her gaze met Dallas's.

McKinney was in profile. "What difference does it make where she—"

"McKinney." Dallas interrupted on a warning tone, tilting his square chin in Sierra's direction.

McKinney turned to Sierra and immediately smiled as if nothing untoward had happened. "*There* you are. We were about to head in for breakfast. Come on and have some eggs."

She gestured to the dining room table that was set with fine china and silverware. A tray of delicious-looking pastries and several covered platters sat in the center while a sideboard held a coffee urn, sugar, cream and a row of generously sized burgundy mugs.

Sierra made it a practice not to shy away from difficult conversations. And she hated to pretend she hadn't overheard when she so obviously had. But, in this case, she decided to follow McKinney's lead.

Dallas had questions about their cover story. Sierra didn't blame him for that. Realistically, it didn't make sense for a trainee ranch hand to be treated like a guest.

"I sure hope you're hungry." McKinney moved the conversation along. "A hearty breakfast is a must around here. And Victor's an amazing cook. You have to try his cinnamon buns."

"The coffee smells great," Sierra said with true enthusiasm. Whatever was in the cards for today, it could only be helped by a strong cup of whatever was brewing.

"Good. Come and sit down," McKinney linked her arm with Sierra's and urged her forward.

Austin trotted down the staircase to join them. "Morning," he greeted everyone and no one.

"Morning," McKinney answered brightly.

Sierra kept her greeting more subdued, expecting Austin might be thinking exactly the same thing as Dallas: What was the new trainee ranch hand doing at the family breakfast table?

Dallas walked around the end of the long table and took

a seat in front of the windows. He didn't look Sierra's way, and it felt like a snub.

"Staff quarters?" She whispered the question into McKinney's ear.

"Don't worry about it," McKinney said as she sat down.

But Sierra *was* worried about it. Her room was far too grand to support their ruse, and she was getting off on entirely the wrong foot with Dallas.

She took the padded leather chair next to McKinney as she considered the predicament.

"Planning on riding today?" Austin asked Dallas as he sat down with his back to the windows.

The corner of Dallas's mouth flexed in what wasn't a smile but couldn't be called a frown either. "Maybe."

"It was just for the one night," Sierra said to Dallas, taking a stab at fixing the problem herself. She was the professional here, and she had to at least try to set the right tone.

He looked her way, his brows slanting together it what seemed like confusion.

But she carried boldly on. "McKinney already told me about the staff quarters."

McKinney knocked her knee against Sierra's.

Sierra shot her a warning look. "I repacked this morning. So, whenever the real room is ready…"

Dallas gave a noncommittal grunt.

"What?" Austin asked, his gaze moving around the three of them, clearly waiting for someone to enlighten him.

"McKinney had Sierra in a guest room last night," Dallas answered his brother.

Austin's brow furrowed. "And?"

"And Dallas objected," McKinney said, reaching for a silver cover and removing it to reveal steaming scrambled eggs.

"I didn't object," Dallas said.

Austin removed the cover from a plate of sausages while Dallas uncovered a dish of crispy hash brown potatoes.

A young man in a buttoned steel blue shirt and gray slacks appeared. He set down a plate of buttered toast, then collected the dish covers from the dining table to set them aside.

"He thinks a guest room's too good for her," McKinney said tartly.

"It is," Sierra said.

Alienating Dallas like this was a very bad strategy. She was surprised McKinney wasn't catching on to that.

"That wasn't my point," Dallas said, his gaze brushing Sierra's for the faintest of seconds.

Despite the discomfort of the atmosphere, the aroma of sausages and melting butter was making her hungrier than usual. It had to be the fresh mountain air.

"Coffee?" the cook offered, looking at McKinney and Sierra.

"Please," McKinney answered.

"Thank you," Sierra said to him.

Although the steaming coffee added to the pleasurable aromas, Sierra was growing more uncomfortable sitting at the family table.

"My point," Dallas drawled to McKinney as the cook left the dining room, "is if she expects to fit in—"

"*She's* sitting right here," McKinney pointed out, giving her brother a hard look.

Dallas glanced guiltily and fleetingly Sierra's way. "I'm saying, it's hard enough for a woman to fit in as a ranch hand without you treating her like a princess."

"I'm moving to the staff quarters today," Sierra repeated firmly, hoping to end the argument. She was relieved when

Austin seemed to move past the conversation by spearing a couple of sausage links and transferring them to his plate.

The sooner this breakfast was over with the better as far as Sierra was concerned.

"Maeve Attenborough," Austin said.

McKinney took a spoonful of scrambled eggs. "Exactly!"

"She's no Maeve Attenborough," Dallas said.

Sierra helped herself to a single sausage. She normally ate a light breakfast, usually yogurt and fruit.

"You have to eat more than that." McKinney added two more sausages to Sierra's plate.

"Who's Maeve Attenborough?" Sierra hoped to take the attention away from herself.

"A ranch hand," Austin answered. He'd loaded up on eggs and hash browns, then added three slices of toast.

"A *female* ranch hand," McKinney interjected, serving Sierra a large spoonful of the eggs.

Dallas gave Sierra an uncompromising look. "Maeve is forty-two, grew up in Jagged Creek and can outride most of the men on the ranch."

Sierra wished she had a counter for that. But she didn't. She'd only ridden a horse once, back in college, the weekend McKinney insisted they take a trail ride together.

But since she wasn't about to volunteer her lack of experience, she stopped talking and took a bite of scrambled eggs.

"She's obviously willing to learn," Austin said, gesturing to Sierra. "You going to refuse that kind of initiative? It's not like we're turning cowboys away at the gate."

Sierra was beginning to like Austin.

"We usually ask for references," Dallas grumbled as he dug into his own breakfast.

"I saw her references," McKinney said.

Sierra schooled her features, careful not to let her surprise show. She wished McKinney wouldn't bluff with quite so much detail. The more they said, the higher their chances of getting tripped up.

"There you go," Austin said, gesturing with his knife as if to close the topic.

Sierra was grateful.

"She should move to the staff quarters," Dallas said. "That was my point."

"I agree." Sierra met his gaze with a steady one of her own. She wanted to show him there were no hard feelings, and she wasn't upset by his suggestion. Getting past the man's defenses was going to be difficult enough already.

"I want you to be comfortable," McKinney said, sounding worried.

"I'll be perfectly comfortable." Before she could stop herself, Sierra put a reassuring hand over McKinney's, then pulled back as she caught Dallas's look of confusion at the overly familiar gesture. "I really, truly appreciate the opportunity to learn," she quickly added.

What Dallas really, truly appreciated was being left alone to get on with his recovery and eventually on with his life. So, when he spotted Sierra at the far side of the main barn, a broom in her hand and a cloud of dust hovering around her knees, he veered right and entered the tack room.

"Howdy, Dallas." Rudy Gains, the stable manager, turned from the island where he was rinsing his hands. He shut off the water and hooked the suspended spray nozzle above the oversize sink.

"Hey, Rudy."

A man Dallas had only seen at a distance, who looked

to be in his early twenties, stopped typing on the laptop that was perched on top of a cabinet and turned to look.

"Help you with something?" Rudy asked as he shook off the water droplets. "Saddle up Jayden?"

"No. I'm good." Dallas was reluctantly giving himself another day before he got back up on his horse. He'd pushed too hard last time. Although he was dying to get back out on the range, he knew if he set himself back, he'd be stuck here even longer.

A young hand sauntered into view at the far end of the rectangular room, hoisting a saddle to settle it on a rack.

Dallas's shoulder hurt just watching the maneuver.

He switched his attention to the computer instead, wondering why they'd set it up in here. The tack room was rife with dirt and dust, not to mention the splash from soaps and oils. "Is this the smartest place for electronics?"

"Inventory," Rudy said with disgust.

The younger man smirked.

"No lip from you," Rudy told him.

"Didn't say a word," the younger man answered, raising his palms in surrender, though clearly not the least bit rattled by Rudy's harsh tone.

"Dallas, this is Ethan. He's a Douglas kid—cousin or something—in for the summer from Denver. Doesn't know a snaffle from a shank, but at least he can make that thing work."

Ethan shook his head with obvious good humor. "Nice to meet you, Dallas."

Dallas gave the man a nod of acknowledgment. Then he glanced around the big, well-lit room at the racks of saddles, bridles and blankets. "You're *counting* the tack?"

Rudy scoffed out a laugh. "I wish."

"Brand, age, condition, maintenance, location and animal," Ethan offered as he clicked the mouse and plunked the keys.

"Why?" Dallas asked.

"One of Austin's grand ideas," Rudy grumbled.

"Efficiency," Ethan said. "You won't overbuy and you'll never run out. Want to see how it works?" He turned the screen Dallas's way.

"Not particularly," Dallas answered. He wasn't expecting to look up his tack on any computer. He'd find what he needed by scanning the racks and shelves, just like he'd always done. "How much is it costing us to record all that?"

"It'll be a savings in the long run," Ethan said.

"Don't get him started," Rudy said.

"Hello?" Sierra's smooth voice interrupted from the doorway, and the unexpected mellow sound zipped along Dallas's spine.

Rudy looked her way. His expression and voice both softened a notch. "Can I help you, ma'am?"

"I'm not a ma'am."

Dallas didn't have to look to know Sierra was smiling. He could hear it clearly in her voice, and he easily pictured it from meeting her last night.

"Ma'am?" Rudy sounded confused now.

"She works here," Dallas explained, catching Ethan's appreciative and captivated expression.

Great. Just what they needed. A budding crush in the tack room.

"I'm a ranch hand trainee," Sierra said, her boots scuffing on the concrete floor as she came fully into the room.

Dallas gave up and turned her way. So much for avoiding her.

"That's a nice idea," Rudy said, sounding like he honestly thought it was.

Not that Dallas could totally blame the man. Even in

faded jeans and scruffy boots, strands of her hair wind-blown around her face, Sierra looked like a magazine cover model. She jazzed up the barn, that was for sure.

"It looked like you had some sweeping to do?" Dallas reminded her. The irritation he was feeling came through in his tone, and uncertainty flashed in her expression.

But she rallied. "I heard your voices, and I'm trying to learn things." She took a few steps toward the island, gazing around.

"You sweep the dirt from the floor and dump it in the corral." Dallas's sarcasm earned him baffled looks from both Rudy and Ethan.

He could see their point. He did sound like a bit of a jerk. But she was here to work, not flash her smile and chitchat with susceptible men. If Ethan was anything to go by, she was going to have a string of admirers from the corral to the cook shack.

McKinney had not thought this through at all.

Sierra seemed not to hear him. She reached for a white gallon-size jug, turning it so the label faced her. Then she glanced around the room as if sizing it up. "Is this where you shampoo the horses?"

"Ma'am?" Rudy was clearly baffled by her peculiar question.

"This is the tack room," Dallas pointed out.

She tilted the label upward. "Conditioner?"

"I know what she means," Ethan said. He left his stool and took a few steps toward the sink and gestured to the dangling spray nozzle. "I thought that at first too."

Dallas had half a mind to call him on the obvious lie.

Ethan might not be an experienced ranch hand, but there was no way he thought they'd bathe horses here.

"Leather conditioner," Rudy told Sierra, adjusting the

angle of his body to read the label with her. "We use it on the tack."

"Oh," Sierra said as if it was a perfectly reasonable answer to a perfectly reasonable question. She set the jug down. "Like I said, I'm here to learn. Maybe I could help someday?"

"Sure," Rudy said.

"You bet," Ethan said over top of him.

"Stick with your assigned chores," Dallas told her. He didn't like throwing cold water on the other two men's obvious desire to hang out with Sierra. But she'd do the work she was assigned. Ranch hands, especially trainee ranch hands, didn't pick their own work.

She looked slightly hurt when she met his gaze. But then she quickly blinked and smiled. "Right. Of course. I guess I'll go back to sweeping up, then."

Ethan wisely returned to the computer and put his head down, obviously not wanting to risk drawing Dallas's ire.

Rudy waited until Sierra left the room before he turned on Dallas.

"What was *that*?"

"She doesn't get special treatment," Dallas responded. "I don't care how pretty she is."

"She's trying to learn."

Dallas frowned.

"You have to respect that," Rudy continued.

"Is there anything, anything at all about her that says ranch hand?" Dallas asked.

Ethan shifted in his seat but didn't join the conversation.

"Don't judge a book by its cover," Rudy said.

"She's a hundred pounds soaking wet," Dallas said.

"I'm not saying we get her hauling hay bales. But she can probably scrub a bridle."

"She can also sweep a floor." Dallas's shoulder tightened with a twinge.

"Whatever you say, boss."

Dallas dialed back his own frustration and moderated his tone. None of this was Rudy's fault. "I'm saying she's fine where she is."

"You bet." Rudy clearly wanted to end the debate as much as Dallas did. "Is there something we can do for you?"

Dallas hesitated over the question. Truth was, he'd ducked in here to avoid seeing Sierra. Fat lot of good it had done him.

"Jayden's cinch seemed a little frayed the other day," he said to cover.

Rudy looked surprised. "Yeah?" A frayed cinch didn't warrant a special trip to the tack room.

"I'll make a note," Ethan offered.

"That's it?" Rudy asked.

"That's it." Dallas gave both men a nod and headed out the door.

Ethan's low voice followed as Dallas walked down the main aisle. "Is he always that much of a hard-ass?"

Dallas halted, his first instinct to turn back around.

"Not always," Rudy answered. "Just lately."

A loud crash and a metallic clatter reverberated through the barn.

Dallas's thoughts went straight to Sierra. He glanced around but couldn't see her, so he broke into a trot.

Pain pulsed through his shoulder with the movement, until he came to the wash bay and stopped. She was sprawled in the middle of the floor, the broom beside her and a bunch of metal buckets scattered around, some slowly rolling in a circle against their rims.

He quickly took in her condition, checking for blood and obvious limb breaks. "*What* happened?"

She grimaced, rubbing her elbow. "I tripped."

"Over what?"

She was out in the middle of an open bay, not an obstacle to be found.

"The broom. I tripped on the broom, and the handle swung over." She gestured to the buckets. "It hit the shelf and brought the buckets down."

Dallas moved closer, his annoyance warring with amusement. "Are you hurt?"

"No."

"Your arm?"

"Is fine. Maybe a bruise." She hoisted herself to her feet.

He started to reach out to help but halted instead, pulling his hand back.

She was a ranch hand, not a maiden in distress. And she'd said herself she wasn't hurt.

"What are you doing in here?" he asked.

"I was walking past." To her credit, she began to restack the buckets. "I looked in and got curious. So, *this* is where you shampoo the horses."

"Yes," he said shortly, not wanting to indulge any favorable feelings toward her.

"That does make more sense," she said in an easy tone while she set the buckets back on the shelf and retrieved the broom.

Her rear was damp from the floor mat, and he found himself staring. He also found himself wanting to stick around and talk to her. That was a clear danger sign.

"So long as you're okay." His tone was clipped as he backed away.

"Maybe I could learn to do that," she said, smiling brightly and with obvious eagerness. "Could you teach me how to shampoo horses?"

It baffled him that she was being so friendly and upbeat. Could she not read his signals?

"Not today," he said, taking a few more backward steps.

"Tomorrow?"

"Sweep," he said. "Just sweep until somebody tells you to stop."

Her expression faltered, but he refused to let it get to him, turning and pacing away before she could ask him for anything else.

Three

Sierra had all she needed in her staff quarters bedroom. It was neat and compact, with a dresser, closet, armchair and a single bed that was surprisingly comfortable for its size. The room had a small but private bathroom, and she'd settled into the space quite easily over the past few days.

"I hate that you're stuck in here," McKinney said, taking a seat in the upholstered chair that sat in a corner near the window. The two women had chatted briefly a few times since Sierra's first day but had kept their contact minimal, not wanting to give away their friendship.

Sierra sat cross-legged on the bed. She was fresh from the shower, dressed in yoga pants and a yellow T-shirt. Her hair was still damp and starting to curl up as it dried on its own. "It's perfectly fine."

McKinney frowned at the plain furniture and at the view through the window of a back parking area lined with pickup trucks. "This wasn't what I planned when I invited you."

"We have to sell our cover story."

McKinney reluctantly nodded, then sat slightly forward. "So? How did it go with Dallas today?"

"He was only in the barn for a few minutes."

McKinney brightened. "And did you talk to him?"

Sierra shook her head. She'd barely spoken to him since that first day when she'd really only made things worse. "He's not warming up to me."

McKinney waved a dismissive hand. "He's not warm to anyone right now. You should have dinner with the family tonight, maybe talk to him there."

"You know I can't do that."

"People join all the time."

"Managers and longtime employees, not trainees."

"No one will notice or care."

Sierra was confident Dallas would notice and care. "You're wrong about that."

"It's casual. Victor's grilling burgers out on the patio with his famous sourdough buns. Lots of extra people will be dropping in and out. Come on over. Let me pour you a glass of wine." McKinney stood.

Having seen the extensive wine cellar, and having a particular weakness for dense homemade sourdough, Sierra couldn't help but be tempted. "I can't go dressed like this."

"Throw on some jeans and a sweater."

"Are you sure it'll be okay?"

McKinney grinned. "I'm positive. It's a great chance for you to talk to Dallas."

"It seems like he's still annoyed with me." Sierra crossed to her small dresser to get a pair of jeans.

"Why? Not that I'm suggesting you did anything," McKinney quickly added. "It's him not you."

"I asked him about cleaning tack and shampooing horses." Sierra stepped into the jeans.

"Oh, the horror!" McKinney put her hand dramatically to her forehead. "And it's bathe. You say bathe a horse."

Sierra pulled a mottled pastel sweater over her head. "So, *that* was my big mistake."

"Like I said, it's not you."

"That was a joke." Sierra smiled to back up her statement. Then she sobered again. "I'm just sorry progress is so slow. I can't even seem to lure him into a conversation."

"We're about to change that." McKinney sounded certain.

Sierra silently vowed to redouble her efforts. At the barbecue he wouldn't be able to send her back to work to end a conversation. She'd have that going for her, at least.

"Maybe tell me more about him," she suggested to McKinney. "What are his hobbies? Does he read? Watch sports?"

"I don't think he reads much. Rodeo was his hobby. And it was definitely his favorite sport."

"Does he have a girlfriend?" As she posed the question, Sierra couldn't help thinking Dallas would be a great catch—handsome, intelligent, hardworking and successful. He must have attracted plenty of women on the rodeo circuit.

She felt a twinge of jealousy thinking about the women in his life. But she quickly quashed it. Personal feelings had no place in her professional services.

"Nobody special that I ever knew about," McKinney said. "He does get plenty of attention out on the rodeo circuit."

"I'm not surprised." Sierra could appreciate the appeal of rugged rodeo cowboys. Dallas was sexy, distractingly sexy—which was the thing she'd just promised not to think about.

She forced herself to move on. "How'd he do in school? Favorite subjects?"

"He was good in math and science, hated English, took all the agricultural electives and liked wood and metal work. Does that help?"

"Some." The list didn't surprise Sierra. She was looking for a mutual interest, something that might draw him into a conversation. So far, she hadn't hit on the right subject.

"You ready?" McKinney asked.

"I am."

As McKinney pulled open the door, she met with the stout, unsmiling fiftyish cook Mrs. Innish. She stepped back in surprise. "Mrs. Innish?"

Mrs. Innish was clearly just as startled to see McKinney. "Ms. Hawkes. I wasn't expecting you."

"We're just on our way out," McKinney responded as if there was nothing strange about her being in Sierra's room.

"I was—" Mrs. Innish's gaze hardened a little as it moved to Sierra. "It was your night to help out in the kitchen."

Sierra had forgotten the assignment, and now she felt terrible. Mrs. Innish was head cook in the staff kitchen. Other staff members took turns to help lighten her load. Sierra hadn't meant to leave her in the lurch.

"I'm so sorry," Sierra said. "I forgot it was my day."

Mrs. Innish's lips flattened. Clearly, she wasn't buying the excuse.

"I need to go help out," Sierra said to McKinney.

"What?" McKinney shot her a look of distress. "You can't."

"I'll come by later."

"But—"

"I don't want to let everyone down." Sierra was trying her best to fit in. Plus, she hated the idea of foisting her work off on Mrs. Innish or someone else.

"You don't need to worry about—"

Sierra's entreating look shut McKinney up.

"I promised I'd help," Sierra said with emphasis.

McKinney's shoulders drooped. "You'll come find me later?"

"I will."

Mrs. Innish raised her chin, looking satisfied by the outcome as she stepped back to the middle of the hallway.

"You better," McKinney warned Sierra before she left, heading down the hallway to the family section of the building.

"You want to be watching that," Mrs. Innish told Sierra as McKinney disappeared through a doorway. "She's your employer, not your friend."

Sierra wished she could correct Mrs. Innish. But she couldn't give herself away.

"I know," she said instead as she shut the bedroom door behind her. "She's a very nice person."

Mrs. Innish marched toward the staff kitchen, where the savory aromas of beef stew and fresh-baked rolls wafted out to meet them. There was an edge to her tone when she spoke. "They're all very nice people until you try to cross that line. And then—"

Sierra was taken aback by the oblique criticism. She couldn't imagine McKinney being anything but polite and professional. Curiosity got the better of her. "Cross what line?"

"The one that separates employees from friends. That'll get you fired in a heartbeat," Mrs. Innish answered, surprising Sierra.

"McKinney fired someone?"

"Not her personally. Other people take care of that sort of thing."

Sierra's curiosity was growing, but she didn't want to gossip about McKinney. Instead of asking another question, she focused on tucking her hair into checkerboard chef's beanie and retrieving a white apron from the cabinet.

"Rolls are already in the oven," Mrs. Innish said.

Sierra pulled the apron over her head and wrapped the apron strings twice around her waist and tied them snugly. She glanced around the kitchen at the partially prepared meal. "How can I help?"

Mrs. Innish began moving salad makings from the refrigerator to the island counter. "My Raymond. He's always been a good boy, friendly to everyone. Everyone liked him."

Sierra pitched in by washing a bowl of plump ripe tomatoes. "You have a son?"

"He worked here most of last summer."

"Oh?"

Mrs. Innish clucked and shook her head. "Until he took a fancy to Ms. Hawkes."

Too late, Sierra realized she'd opened herself up for more gossip. "Shall I slice the cucumbers?" She positioned a cutting board and reached for the deep green vegetables.

"Boom, bam, out the door. It was Garrett himself that did the deed."

"I'm sorry," Sierra mumbled. She didn't want to hear the details. "Is there a good knife for slicing?" She glanced around for a butcher's block.

Mrs. Innish held a head of leaf lettuce under the streaming faucet.

Sierra spotted the knives on another counter and retrieved one of them.

"How many should I cut?" She checked the rind to see

if the cucumbers needed peeling, deciding the skins felt tender enough. Cucumber rind was chock-full of antioxidants and vitamin K. It was better for everyone's health to leave it on.

"It was a class thing between them," Mrs. Innish added. "Sure as I'm standing here."

Sierra compressed her lips and took a beat. She didn't want to alienate Mrs. Innish, but she couldn't let the comments stand either.

Voices sounded through the door to the staff sitting room. The chatter and laughter grew quickly close, and the swinging door opened.

"Love the smell of that stew," a man said as several people piled through the doorway to surround the big kitchen dining table.

Mrs. Innish went silent, and Sierra breathed a sigh of relief.

On the back patio overlooking the lighted pond and brook, Dallas was glad to have dinner over and done with. He loved Victor's famous burgers as much as anyone, but he'd had about as much cheerful togetherness as he could stand. He wanted to be alone now, take the fake smile off his face, let his guard down and admit his shoulder was throbbing with every heartbeat.

He'd ridden Jayden again today, and there was a painkiller with his name on it back in his room. He was down to one every twenty-four hours now, and this one was going to let him get a good night's sleep, hopefully a dreamless one.

He polished off a tumbler of soda and lime as the lights came up one by one around the patio. The feature staircase, rock wall perimeter and the waterfall across the pond become more prominent and spectacular as night fell. He hoped everyone else enjoyed it, but his evening was over.

He headed toward the kitchen to drop his empty glass on his way upstairs.

"I tried really hard to get out of the conversation," Sierra's voice stopped him in his tracks.

"Who did she say got fired?" McKinney asked, sounding puzzled.

The two women were screened by a stone pillar.

"Her son Raymond."

Dallas's nostrils flared at the name.

"There was something strange in the way she said it," Sierra continued.

"Sierra," Dallas firmly interrupted the conversation, taking the few strides that brought him to the women. "I didn't expect to see you here."

Both women looked his way, McKinney puzzled, Sierra apprehensive—not that he blamed her given his attitude. Still, he wouldn't change how coolly he'd treated her. She didn't belong here, and he didn't belong anywhere near her.

"Got a minute?" he asked her anyway. Priority one was to stop this conversation before it went any further. He'd figure out how to be unfriendly again afterward.

"Something wrong?" she asked, looking concerned.

"I invited her here tonight," McKinney said staunchly. "I'm not kicking her out."

"Sure, I've got a minute." Sierra's demeanor switched to friendly on a dime, and she smiled at him.

McKinney hesitated a second longer, but then seemed to willingly accept the situation. "Catch you later, then," she said to Sierra. "Make sure you grab a glass of wine. The Burgundy is to die for."

"Sure," Sierra answered, but it was clear she didn't mean it.

It was unusual for people to turn something down from his dad's cellar. He wondered if she wasn't a drinker, or if she didn't care for wine. Then he told himself to stop wondering and focus on the problem.

"Can we?" he asked, gesturing to the firepit one level lower than the main patio and next to the pond. It was raised and round, constructed of stones and mortar, ablaze right now with wood and surrounded by eight empty Adirondack chairs.

"What's up?" she asked easily as they descended the five stairs.

Dallas didn't see any point in beating around the bush. "I'd rather you didn't talk to McKinney about Raymond Innish." He stopped as they came into the heat and crackle of the fire.

The night was still, and the fire hot, so the thin smoke rose straight up into the blue-black sky.

Sierra turned, her eyes narrowing in obvious confusion in the flickering amber glow. "I hope you know I wasn't gossiping."

"The guy had a crush on her," Dallas explained.

"So you fired him?" Sierra sounded both surprised and disapproving.

"Not for having a crush on her, no. He was slacking off, finding ways to hang around her instead of getting his work done. Not that she noticed."

"You couldn't have given him a warning or something?"

"His poor performance caused the foreman to look more closely at his job application. Turned out he forged a letter of reference."

Sierra's mouth formed a silent "oh." She gazed contemplatively into the fire then. She was pretty in profile, especially in the soft light, far too pretty for Dallas's peace of mind. His attraction grew stronger every time he saw her.

"You didn't want to embarrass McKinney," Sierra said softly.

"There didn't seem to be any point in that. And his mother's a valued long-standing ranch employee. All in all, it seemed better to keep it low-key."

"Mrs. Innish thinks you considered him unworthy of McKinney."

Dallas gave a shrug, sending pain flashing through his shoulder. "He's an adult. It's up to him to be honest with his mother. Though I do hope he's learned his lesson."

"Your shoulder hurts." Sierra had obviously seen his wince.

"It's fine."

She gave a little smile and a shake of her head. "You're an adult too, Dallas. It's up to you to be honest with me."

He frowned, not liking the way she turned the tables.

"McKinney said you were bucked off in the rodeo," she continued.

"It happens," he said matter-of-factly.

"I've seen bronc riding. Not in person or anything. But I've seen it on TV. You know, the highlights. It looks dangerous."

"Never been to a rodeo?" he asked, looking to turn the conversation away from himself, onto her instead.

She smiled at that, and there was amusement in her eyes.

He liked that he'd made her smile. He wanted to do it again. He wanted to do a whole bunch of things right now, including drawing her into his arms and kissing her.

"I grew up in Carmel, California," she said.

He tamped down his wayward feelings. "Not notably a hotbed of rodeoing."

"Not notably."

"Since you're a rancher now, you might want to take one in."

"I'm a rancher?"

"Rancher wannabe." He couldn't help making the joke.

"Hey, cowboy. I sweep a mean stall."

"You tripped over your broom."

She winced. "Fair point. Got any tips?"

He wanted to say yes. He wanted to offer to help her, to teach her the fundamentals, to give himself an excuse to spend more time with her. But he'd indulged his attraction as far as he dared.

He hardened himself, easing away, suddenly realizing how close they'd drawn to each other. "Watch your feet."

"I meant about ranching, not tripping."

"Like I said, there are plenty of good teachers around here."

She gave him a look that said she had his number. "And you're busy."

"I'm busy."

"Got it."

He felt like the rudest of jerks. "I have a lot to do."

"I understand."

"Do you?"

She unexpectedly put her hand on his arm. It was covered by his shirtsleeve, but the touch shot through the cotton fabric to embed itself in his skin.

"It's okay, Dallas."

He wasn't looking for her forgiveness, didn't want her forgiveness and was annoyed that she'd offered it.

"I know it's okay," he said tersely, pulling his arm from under her hand.

She looked offended for a second, and he told himself he was glad. Maybe now she'd stay out of his way.

"Good night, Sierra," he said and turned sharply away.

Four

Sierra rested the wheelbarrow of soiled straw on the floor next to the open barn door and inhaled a breath of fresh air. She spotted Dallas in the distance for the first time in several days.

He was on horseback and looked good riding the tawny-colored animal, its proud head and dark mane in relief against the distant mountains. Dallas's spine was ramrod straight, his hips deep in the saddle, his Stetson low on his head. One arm hung loosely by his side, brushing the faded jeans above his scuffed cowboy boots as he spoke to his brother Austin and a third, older ranch hand.

His image hit her on an emotional level, reigniting the surge of attraction she'd felt the night of the barbecue. She'd fought it then, but right now she let the compelling sensation slide over her skin like warm silk. He was one magnificent man.

Since she couldn't read lips, she had no idea what they

were saying. She wished she was close enough to overhear. She'd love to be a fly on the wall for Dallas's unguarded conversations.

Sure, she could tell he was aloof and stoic. And from what McKinney had shared, Sierra knew he was highly frustrated with his injury and with being in physical pain. And, given his reluctance to help her, he clearly wasn't cut out to be a teacher. She found herself smiling at the idea. Patience was not his strong suit.

The conversation among the cowboys ended. Austin and the other man rode away up the hill. Instead of following them, Dallas looked her way.

She took a quick step back to the shadows but realized she wasn't what had caught his attention. He was focused on two young boys in a corral off the side of the barn.

She recognized them as Albert and Zeke. She knew they were the oldest of the staff members' children, although she wasn't exactly clear on which kids belonged to whom just yet.

The boys were around ten years old, and they were struggling to put a saddle on a small horse.

Dallas walked his own horse to the edge of the corral and dismounted. It looked like he was going to help the boys, but instead he draped his forearms on the second-highest rail. He said something, and they both looked up.

The lanky, blond-haired Albert asked a question.

Dallas answered. Whatever he said caused them to set down the saddle and trot away.

Dallas lifted a foot and braced it on the bottom rail, waiting patiently.

Albert and Zeke soon jogged back, each wearing a helmet and carting a wooden box between them.

Dallas smiled at their efforts, and Sierra's chest gave a little lift.

After further instructions and hand gestures from Dallas, the dark-haired, stockier Zeke set the box down next to the very patient horse. Albert stepped up on it. Then Zeke hoisted the saddle to Albert, who managed to push the saddle into place on the horse's back. The two kids then beamed with pride.

Dallas continued with the instructions while the boys secured the saddle, then he finally hoisted himself over the fence to check their work.

Afterward, the pair rushed off again, then returned with a second horse.

Sierra heard voices and footfalls echo inside the barn and quickly picked up where she'd left off with the wheelbarrow. She had work to finish. But it had been educational watching Dallas with the boys.

He wasn't nearly as hard-nosed as he pretended to be, she mused as she dumped the straw. Or else he had a soft spot for kids—which she wouldn't have expected. Also, it would seem, when someone truly needed his help, he didn't walk away.

That realization got her thinking while she clipped a lead rope onto Cedric's bridle to move him from his stall.

Cedric was a tall elderly Percheron Morgan cross. Placid and steady, he was one of the few horses Sierra was completely comfortable around. He gave a low whinny next to her ear. She gave him a rub on the neck and a scratch behind the ear. He leaned in closer, clearly enjoying the contact.

"You're such a good boy," she said soothingly. "Want to go outside for a while?"

Cedric and his best friend Apple, whom Sierra had learned was an Appaloosa, were retired, except for the occasional rides for children.

Apple gave a higher-pitched whinny as Sierra led Cedric out of his stall.

"Don't worry, you're next," Sierra reassured the mare.

As she started down the wide center aisle toward a side door that would lead to an empty corral, a plan formulated in her mind. She realized she'd been coming at Dallas the wrong way. The trick wasn't to politely ask for his help. The trick was to truly need his help.

She smiled at her own brilliance as Dallas's voice sounded from the direction of the tack room. A concrete idea took shape inside her head. It was a good idea. One might even say an inspired idea. She looked up at the horse, and he blinked at her with his big brown eyes.

"How would you feel about a bath?" she asked him.

He didn't answer, but he looked like he'd be agreeable to just about anything.

She wouldn't have to give him an entire bath. If she took the horse into the wash bay and fumbled around for a few minutes, maybe made some obvious noise about it, she might attract Dallas's attention. If she got his attention and looked inept enough, he might feel obligated to help her out.

It would undoubtedly frustrate him, but if she could get him to stay in one place for a few minutes and talk to her, she'd at least be ahead of where she was now.

"Let's do it," she said to Cedric and altered her course.

Cedric came along easily, not shying in the least at going into the wash bay and turning around.

Clearly, he'd done this before and knew the drill. That was encouraging.

Positioning Cedric on a black rubber mat positioned below the hose, she spotted a ring on the wall. Perfect. She tied off the lead rope to keep the horse in place.

She rubbed Cedric's neck again, scratching behind each

of his ears and along his nose, trying to bond before she sprayed him with the hose.

"Are you ready for this?" she asked, moving to his side and rubbing his withers the way she'd seen McKinney do.

Cedric stilled, and she rubbed again. He stretched out his neck, looking like he was in horsey heaven.

"You like that?" she asked and massaged a little harder.

His muscles felt tense under her hand, reminding her of her human clients, and it was clear he liked the increased pressure.

She couldn't imagine what a retired horse would have to be stressed about living in a place like the Hawkes ranch. But clearly Cedric was carrying some tension in his shoulders.

She switched to both hands, using her thumbs and the heels of her hands to look for problem points.

Cedric shifted his feet, shook his head, then leaned into the massage.

"Who would have guessed," she said to him.

After a few minutes, she moved to his other side, using the same process.

He closed his eyes and let out a shuddering breath.

"We're going to be great friends," she told him. "You might be big and nonverbal. But wow. It's easy to tell how much you appreciate this."

Dallas's voice sounded in the distance again. He was too far away for her to make out the words, but he was obviously in a conversation with someone. It reminded her that the point of all this was to attract his attention and maybe get his help.

She didn't want to bang around and startle Cedric out of his almost hypnotic bliss. But she had to do something. She raised her voice. "This is going to be great," she said cheerfully.

The horse blinked and gave his head another shake.

"You'll feel so clean and refreshed when we're done." She paused to listen and heard the men's conversation continue.

She turned on the hose, selecting a lukewarm setting. The hose and tank made a chugging sound that she hoped might draw attention. She started at Cedric's shoulder, wetting it down. As water splashed and dripped to the floor, she realized rubber boots would have served her well. Or maybe a pair of hip waders.

Cedric seemed to like the water pressure, so she sprayed over his back and up his neck to his ears, deciding to forget about how wet she'd end up before this was over.

She shut off the water and paused, listening for Dallas's voice. The conversation continued.

She abandoned the hose for a large shampoo bottle sitting on a supply shelf.

"In for a penny," she said to Cedric in a loud voice while awkwardly squirting shampoo along the length of his back.

As the shampoo lathered up, she had an inspiration. She could sing a lot louder than she could talk. And Cedric might like the music, even if her voice was mediocre at best.

The only appropriate song she could think of was about a rubber ducky. She started soft, then increased the volume until she was belting it out as she lathered Cedric from neck to tail.

He seemed as happy to be shampooed as he'd been to get a massage.

The suds began to turn brown, telling her the process was working.

"*What* are you doing?" Dallas's voice startled her.

She whipped her head around to find him standing there, feet planted apart, arms crossed over his chest. In her zeal, she'd forgotten about trying to attract his attention.

"Washing Cedric," she answered brightly, hoping she looked inept at it.

"How much shampoo did you use?"

"I think it's working great. Look at all that dirt I'm getting out."

"You have to use crossties for this." Dallas grabbed a lead rope from a hook outside and marched forward, clipping it from Cedric's bridle to a ring on the opposite wall of the wash stall. "You've got the soap way too close to his eyes. And look at that hose? He could easily step on it or get tangled."

Up to her elbows in suds, her entire front soaking wet, and listening to the litany of her mistakes, Sierra knew she had Dallas's attention now. She hoped she hadn't blown past ineptness and into ridiculousness.

"He's been really cooperative," she said.

"You're lucky it was Cedric."

"I knew it was Cedric. I know he's a good boy."

"He's fifteen hundred pounds." Dallas retrieved a sponge, dampened it and carefully wiped the suds from around the horse's face.

Sierra had a bad moment as she contemplated what might have happened if the soap had stung Cedric's eyes. She swallowed the burst of guilt and alarm.

Dallas finished with the sponge and took in her appearance. His scowl was deep, and she knew she'd messed up.

Her shoes were soggy, and a stream of shampoo oozed its way down her wet thigh.

"Let me guess," he said, sounding more resigned than angry. "Spur-of-the-moment decision?"

Dallas's frustration with Sierra was short-lived.

He had to admire her spirit and composure in the face of his criticism. But he wanted to discourage her from plunging into unsafe situations. If she kept it up, someone could get hurt.

He took in the grimy mess of soap and suds and guessed what had happened. "Did you not brush him out first?"

Her look of confusion was her answer.

"Next time ask for help," he said.

Her composure slipped. "I *have* been asking you for help."

"I don't mean from me." Okay, he'd made that abundantly clear.

After the brief pause, she continued rubbing suds into Cedric's coat. "McKinney has given me some advice. I don't really want to bother Rudy."

"But you don't mind bothering me." He sponged Cedric's face a second time to make sure the soap stayed out of his eyes.

"McKinney said you were very experienced."

"Plenty of people around here are experienced."

"And you're one of them."

"I feel like we're going in a circle."

She stepped away from Cedric. "You might want to step out of the way." She took the hose from the holder.

"Use a low-pressure flow," he warned her, resisting the urge to step in and take over. The more she learned hands on, the safer she'd be.

"I will."

"Dial the nozzle to the left."

She turned the nozzle, looking close to read the settings.

He stepped forward and lifted it from her hands. "Don't do that."

She jerked in surprise.

"There might be pressure built up in the hose. You could hurt yourself." It was a bit of an exaggeration, but you never pointed a pressure nozzle straight in your face.

"Thanks," she said.

He checked her expression, wondering if she was being sarcastic. But she seemed genuinely appreciative of the advice.

He pointed the nozzle away from them and turned the dial. Sure enough, a spurt of water came out as he stopped on the right position.

He handed it back and opened the tap. "It's going to take you forever to rinse out all that soap."

"Better get started, then," she said and directed the spray on Cedric.

Dallas backed away to avoid getting wet. "You need to be dressed right for this job."

"I'll remember that for next time." She at least knew enough to start at the top and work her way down.

"Keep the hose away from his hooves," Dallas advised.

She moved the hose to a safe position and continued spraying off the suds.

Cedric stood placidly while she worked.

"I saw you out in the corral with the boys," she said, moving the stream of water along his upper body. "You seemed very patient with them."

"They're getting to the we'll-do-it-by-ourselves stage."

"You remember being their age?" she asked easily, her concentration focused on Cedric's haunches.

He did. But the memories were bittersweet, and he didn't spend much time dwelling on them. His mom had still been around back then. It was long before the accident that took her life.

"Not much," he said to get out of the discussion.

"Were you riding by then?"

"At ten years old?" He couldn't help but chuckle at the question.

"I'll take that as a yes."

"I was up on a horse at four."

She smiled, and it gave her an inner glow. The essence was soft, like evening sunshine. "Impressive."

"Horses are a part of life around here."

"I can see that. You have a favorite?"

"I usually ride Jayden when I'm at the ranch." He almost listed off his rodeo horses, but he stopped himself. Those memories were best left alone right now too.

"And for the rodeo?" she asked, looking his way, giving him the uncanny feeling she was reading his thoughts.

He shrugged, remembering too late it hurt his shoulder.

She waited.

"There were a lot of different horses," he said.

"McKinney mentioned you roped as well as rode broncos. I thought that took a highly trained horse."

"It does."

"But you have a lot of them? Highly trained?" Her tone was even, but he felt like she was on a mission rather than just making conversation.

He pointed to Cedric's shoulder. "You missed a spot."

"Oops." She redirected the spray.

"What made you decide to try ranching?" he asked to turn the tables.

"Change of pace," she said.

"From?" he prompted.

She stepped back and surveyed the horse.

Cedric looked rinsed to him, so he shut off the tap.

"Working with people," she said, coiling the hose.

He gave in to his urge this time and lifted the heavy hose from her hands. "You don't like people?"

"They disappoint me sometimes."

"How?" he asked, his gaze catching on her jewel-blue eyes.

The coiled hose between them, they were standing face-to-face.

"Do they disappoint you too?" she asked, sidestepping ever so neatly.

"People are predictable." He excluded Sierra from that statement. Who could have predicted she'd up and bathe a horse?

"I really wish they were," she countered.

"But you don't agree?" He was intrigued to hear more.

"Not in the ways it counts."

"How does it count?"

She seemed to think about that for a minute. "Honor, I guess. Trustworthiness."

"I think most people are honorable. Most of the time, anyway. When they're not, you can usually spot their motivation."

She smiled, and his chest tightened with a hitch. "You do know that's a good sign, right?"

He didn't understand. "What's a good sign?"

"Honorable people assume others are honorable."

"And you don't?" He couldn't help but tease her with the irony. "What does that say about you, Sierra?"

She didn't answer, but he could see the amusement in her eyes. She didn't seem to mind a joke at her expense. He considered that a good sign where it came to her character.

Silence settled between them.

She should have looked like a drowned rat with her damp hair stringy and messy around her face, stray soap bubbles clinging above one ear and her blue cotton shirt plastered to her skin. Instead, she looked sexy, so very sexy. Her cheeks were flushed from exertion, and she had an enigmatic half smile on her pretty face.

He was overcome once again with the urge to kiss her. The urge was stronger and even more unsettling this time, since they were alone here with nothing to stop them.

Her eyes darkened with awareness, going from jewel to indigo.

"You're soaking wet," he said, though it was totally irrelevant.

"To the skin," she responded on a whisper.

The sultry sound amped up his desire.

She didn't back down from the energy building between them. If anything, she swayed toward him.

He stroked the pad of his thumb along the curve of her jaw. Her skin was smooth and damp, warm under the layer of water.

She drew in a breath, her lips softening and parting.

He inched forward and slowly smoothed her hairline, settling his hand intimately across the back of her neck.

She tilted her chin, and he angled his lips, leaning down in slow motion. The voice of caution in his brain grew dimmer with every inch.

Her sweet breath puffed as his lips came down.

Sensation rolled through him like thunder. His hand tightened, pulling her closer, settling her lips more firmly against his.

She gave a little moan.

He reached for her waist, and the hose dropped to the floor.

"Ouch," she cried as the nozzle clattered.

He jerked back. "Are you okay?"

"It hit my foot."

"I'm sorry."

She seemed to suddenly realize what they'd done. Her eyes went round, and her jaw went lax as she pulled away. "No. I'm sorry. That shouldn't have—I didn't mean—"

He shook his head. "Not your fault. I kissed you."

He kicked himself for doing it. It had been completely out of line. But she'd filled his mind in the most soothing way. While they kissed, the usual litany of painful emotions had slipped quietly away.

She glanced furtively around the barn now, clearly worried that someone might have seen them together.

There was nobody around.

"That shouldn't have happened," she said, sounding slightly panicked.

"You're right. I know." He was back to his senses.

"Can we just forget it?"

"Absolutely." He doubted he could pull that off, but he'd give it his best shot. At the very least, he could pretend to forget about it.

"Good." She gave an awkward nod and reached toward the floor.

"I'll get that." He beat her to the hose.

She moved aside, putting a hand on Cedric's flank as if she needed to brace herself.

"I'm sorry," he said again, knowing he was the one who'd made the move.

She might have kissed him back, but he'd been the instigator. He simply hadn't been able to help himself.

She waved away his apology. "It's forgotten. We—" Her expression contorted. "It was a heat-of-the-moment thing. Could have happened to anyone."

"Right," he lied. He'd never impulsively kissed a woman that way. His kisses up to now had been planned and purposeful.

He wanted to ask if she impulsively kissed men. But it was none of his business. And he didn't want to think about the other men she might have kissed.

Dallas forced his mind back to business. "Let him stand and dry for a while."

She nodded. "Sure."

He forced his feet to move toward the wash bay exit.

"There's a stack of towels in the cupboard across the aisle if you want to speed it up."

"Thanks." Her voice sounded small.

He paused and looked back. "You okay?"

"Fine." She smoothed her messy hair. "Great."

He suddenly couldn't leave it like this, not without knowing for sure how she felt.

He walked back over to her, watching closely. "I didn't pressure you into anything, did I? I mean—" He wasn't sure how to phrase the question.

She caught on right away. "Because you're my boss?"

"I'm not your boss. But, yeah, I'm a Hawkes."

She shook her head in denial. "It was me too. Don't blame yourself."

He did blame himself. Even if she had been willing, he'd foolishly given in to impulse. He knew better than that.

She locked gazes with him. "It really is okay, Dallas. Let's chalk it up to…" She gave a helpless little shrug. "I don't know."

"The romantic surroundings?" He tried to lighten the mood.

She rewarded him with a more relaxed smile, then gestured to herself. "My alluring outfit?"

He chuckled to go along with the joke. But alluring didn't even come close. His gaze did an involuntary sweep of her, memorizing every beautiful inch, knowing the picture would be stuck in his brain for days and days to come.

Five

Sierra discovered it was easy to catch a ride from the satellite barns and corrals back to the main ranch house. All
she had to do was start walking. Within minutes, someone
would come along in a pickup and stop to give her a lift.

Today it was Ethan. The twenty-something computer
tech was living in the bunkhouse, but he immediately offered to take her the extra half mile to the main house, just
like everyone always did.

Ethan was friendly and easygoing. Born and raised in
Denver, he was in the process of changing careers and
studying computer systems at Metropolitan State. Several
of his extended family members worked or had worked on
the Hawkes ranch, and he was here for the summer, experiencing ranch life while he helped modernize their operation.

Ethan was friendly enough, even slightly flirtatious.
But she was careful to keep things low-key between them.
It was too soon after her breakup to think about dating.

Plus, there was the memory of Dallas's kiss.

It was odd that she hadn't felt conflicted by that kiss—at least not from the perspective of Roger. In fact, it had obliterated her memories of Roger. Not that Roger's kisses had held much passion in those last weeks, maybe even in the past months. She struggled to figure out how far back she had to go to recall true passion.

On the other hand, there was no denying her passionate reaction to Dallas. They might as well have been naked, pressed together head to toe, maybe tangled in a set of soft sheets with candles flickering and Michael Bublé or Enrique Iglesias wafting in the background.

"Am I boring you?" Ethan interrupted her thoughts as they turned from the gravel road to the smooth pavement that circled the ranch house.

"No. Not at all." She quickly smiled in his direction, struggling to remember what they'd been talking about.

He looked decidedly skeptical.

She widened her smile. "You were talking about electronic monitoring."

His expression turned happy and a little relieved by what seemed to be a correct guess. "Yes. With a signal booster and using the satellite array, we can extend wireless up the fence line. That'll keep the cowboys on the network miles from the homestead."

"They must appreciate your innovation," she said as he pulled the pickup to a stop near a back door of the main house.

"Austin does," Ethan answered. "Rudy, not so much. And Dallas. Well, I think he'd prefer to stay in the 1990s."

Sierra paused while reaching for the door handle. "You think?" Her interest perked up at the mention of Dallas. It hadn't occurred to her to try to get some insight on him from Ethan. "He doesn't strike me as old-fashioned."

Ethan coughed out a laugh at that. "You should hear him argue with Austin."

"About technology?" Sierra was taking mental notes.

"About anything. 'Nothing wrong with the way it's always been done' is one of his favorite phrases."

"Really." A mental barrier against progress wasn't an unusual trait, and she'd file that knowledge away.

Sometimes people were holding on to a happier past. Often, they were intimidated by an uncertain future. Dallas definitely had an uncertain future.

"I guess it's hard to come home to ten years of change," Ethan said.

Sierra knew Dallas had been rodeoing for most of the past decade. He'd left home at eighteen and only returned to the ranch during long breaks in the schedule. And those long breaks had become fewer and farther between.

"Anything else?" Sierra prompted. She was thinking now that she might subtly quiz a few of the other ranch staff members about Dallas. Rudy seemed like a particularly good place to start.

Ethan stretched an arm across the bench seat of the truck and smiled. "Not about Dallas."

Sierra took that as a cue to leave. The last thing she wanted to do was encourage Ethan on any romantic front. "Thanks for the ride," she said cheerfully, lifting the latch and pushing the passenger door open. "I guess I'll probably see you tomorrow."

His smile dimmed slightly. "Sure."

"Bye-bye." She hopped out of the truck and shut the door behind herself, hoping she hadn't offended him. She'd like to be friends, but that was all she wanted.

She'd taken to using a back door closest to the main kitchen because it was convenient to her room. Utilitarian and practical, it led to a foyer lined with coat hooks and shelves, with a wraparound bench and spaces for boots underneath. It opened directly into a laundry room, so there was a deep sink, soap and towels available for initial washing up.

Dusty from the barns, she pushed up her sleeves and headed for the sink.

Austin's voice carried through a closed door from the family kitchen. "It is smart. And it *does* make sense."

"Slow down," McKinney said with a note of caution. "Let's walk our way through this."

"We already know whose side you're on," Dallas came back dryly.

Sierra paused, thinking about Ethan's assessment of Dallas. It sure sounded like they were debating progress and innovation.

"It's progress," McKinney said, reflecting Sierra's theory.

"We have to move with the times," Austin said.

"I don't know why you're objecting," Garrett's deep voice sounded.

Sierra startled a little at the sound of the senior family member. Garrett was aloof and struck her as judgmental. She'd made sure to give him a wide berth, sensing it would be easy to get on his bad side.

"We're large," he continued in his gravelly voice. "We're diverse. Your sister's a shining example."

"It's hard, heavy work," Dallas said on a bitter note.

Sierra waited, wondering about the specifics of the conversation. Then she wondered if they might be discussing a suggestion from Ethan. If so, she hoped it went his way. He seemed eager to have the ranch use his innovation ideas.

"She stays," McKinney said emphatically.

"If it comes to a vote," Austin said.

"Is *that* where we are?" Dallas demanded. "Arguing about a trainee."

With a jolt, Sierra realized they were talking about her.

"We argue about everything these days," McKinney said dryly.

"McKinney," Garrett warned.

In the following silence, Sierra could hear her own heartbeat. The laundry room was separated from the main kitchen by a sliding pocket door. And it was a few inches ajar, so the voices had flowed freely.

She slunk silently backward.

"I'd prefer a consensus," Garrett said.

"And I'd prefer experienced ranch hands," Dallas retorted.

"She's learning," McKinney said. "Everybody has to learn sometime."

"She's what?" Dallas asked. "Twenty—"

"Three," McKinney said. "Same age as me."

There was a moment of silence.

"I read her résumé," McKinney clarified.

"Well, I didn't," Dallas said. "Did you? Or did you?" It was clear the staccato questions were directed to Austin and Garrett.

Sierra retreated to the foyer, not knowing whether to be angry or heartsick over Dallas trying to get her fired.

Their kiss had obviously meant nothing to him.

Maybe he kissed women like that all the time. Maybe he'd pegged her as a flirt, acted on impulse and regretted it now. The thought was intensely embarrassing. Could she fall any lower in his esteem?

She lowered herself to the bench and peeled off her boots. There was no good interpretation of his words. At the very least, he considered her an inept ranch hand who wasn't worth keeping.

Fine.

She stowed her boots and stuffed her feet into a pair of mesh-top slip-ons. It was probably time to leave anyway. She wasn't going to make any progress with Dallas under these circumstances.

"There's no need to be rash." Garrett's commanding voice suddenly boomed.

Sierra froze for a second. Then she took a beat.

He obviously wasn't talking to her.

She took another beat, thinking maybe she should take his advice anyway.

There was no need for her to be rash, especially since Dallas wasn't completely wrong—at least about her ineptitude. Her sense of professionalism kicked back in, telling her to rise to the challenge. Whatever Dallas might think of her, she was here as his wellness coach.

She could move past the kiss. And she was only sweeping stalls and washing horses as a cover story. She'd tried hard, but it was true she was still a beginner. And what did it matter how she handled ranch work anyway? The only relevant measure was the progress she'd made helping him.

To be brutally honest, that progress was zero. But she was gaining helpful information by the day, even by the hour. Soon she'd be able to make suggestions to McKinney about helping her brother. And she owed that to her friend. She owed that to the entire Hawkes family, since they'd been feeding, housing, even paying her all this time.

She rose to her feet, vowing to get past her hurt feelings. It was time to quit worrying about Dallas's opinion and behave like a professional.

Dallas usually avoided the winding drive down Brighton Road to get to the town of Jagged Creek. He preferred to hop over to the highway on the northeast connector road, even though it was longer. But today, the connector road was blocked by a mudslide, caused by a flash flood high in the mountains.

It happened sometimes. And the little-used road from the Hawkes ranch wasn't a government priority. It got cleared when it got cleared.

As he approached the one-lane bridge at Goat Canyon, he turned up the music, letting the playlist on his phone bounce off the doors and windows of the cab's interior. The deep base throbbed through his brain, and he kept his eyes front as he passed the spot where his mother's car had spun off the road.

Fifteen minutes later, the town came into view.

The newly built Oberfeld Hotel now dominated the landscape, blotting the iconic Field and Feed Store from view. They'd cut a wide swath of trees along the banks of Jagged Creek, improving the view and making room for future landscaping.

Local residents were excited about the project, since the hotel would bring many more tourists into town. Three trendy cafés had sprung up, and the tone of the town had started to change. Western shirts, blue jeans and cowboy boots had been replaced by khakis, bright white sneakers and crew neck sweaters.

Some of the shops along Main Street were stocking their shelves with tourist trinkets—coffee mugs, T-shirts and belt buckles. It felt like an imitation ranching town these days instead of an authentic one.

He'd been approached by one of the local stores on a deal to use his name and likeness bareback bronc riding. Like notoriety was what he needed in his life.

He angle-parked against the sidewalk beneath the red awning of the Cactus Spur. It was too early in the afternoon for a beer, but the Spur served a great cup of coffee and brought fresh doughnuts in daily from Maggie's Bake Shop down the block.

A few cowboys would be hanging around the place right now. He could catch up on news from the surrounding ranches before heading down to Boots and Blues for a new pair of harness boots, and maybe a couple of shirts and some jeans. Shopping wasn't his strong suit. He generally wore things until they fell apart.

As his truck engine fell to silence, Dallas spotted the closed sign on the glass door. He checked his watch, not that it told him anything new. The Cactus Spur opened at noon, and it was well past that.

Not quite believing what he was seeing, he stepped outside, slamming the driver's door behind him and pacing across the sidewalk.

The closed sign was handwritten on paper curling at the edges. It was taped to the inside of the door. *Until Further Notice* it said in smaller print.

Dallas glanced up and down the street, baffled as to why a business as popular as the Cactus Spur would be closed. Were they renovating? They hadn't renovated in over forty years, and nobody minded. He didn't see why they'd start now.

He tried the door, but it was locked, and annoyance bubbled up inside him. He'd been looking forward to coffee and a Maggie's doughnut. Most of all, he'd been looking forward to some familiar faces and interesting ranching news. It was one of the few reasons to tolerate the hubbub of town.

Hands on his hips, he stepped back.

"Closed down a month ago," a gravelly male voice said from behind him.

Dallas turned to see seventy-year-old Wilson Camry tilt tip his Stetson up on his forehead.

"Shame that," Wilson said as he stepped up even with Dallas.

"I'll say," Dallas agreed. "What happened?"

"Dozer sold out. Said he was retiring."

"Sold out to who?"

Wilson gave a shrug. "Some gal. Word is she's opening a boo-teak." His tone was derisive as he drew out the word.

"Well, that stinks." Dallas didn't know what type of boutique it was going to be, but it was a safe bet it wasn't one that sold draft beer, peanuts in the shell and juicy burgers that dripped all over a cowboy's plate. "Where's everybody drinking these days?"

"Some at the Spring Wall and some at the Cell."

Dallas frowned at both options. The Spring Wall wouldn't welcome dusty cowboys, while the Cell was most famous for its low-brow clientele and occasional after-midnight brawls.

"I was looking for coffee and a doughnut," he said.

"Maggie's." Wilson stated the obvious.

"And conversation," Dallas said. He didn't expect to find that at Maggie's in the middle of an afternoon.

"Heard you were back," Wilson said. "Heard you got your arm twisted up."

"My shoulder," Dallas said, involuntarily tightening his muscle around the pain.

"Shame that."

"Thanks." Dallas acknowledged the gruff sympathy. "I'll be back out there soon."

He used the word *soon* in the broadest possible sense. As the days slipped past, a complete recovery seemed further and further away.

He'd been optimistic at first, while his doctor had been more cautionary. But doctors were like that. And Dallas figured he knew his body better than anybody. Now… He wasn't so sure.

"Cowboy up," Wilson said.

Dallas gave a curt nod of agreement. "How are things out at the Circle Seth?"

"Fair to middlin'. Dry year. Taxes are up. Beef prices low. But my arthritis likes the heat."

Dallas nodded to acknowledge the man's frustrations, feeling empathy for Wilson's health problems. He'd never much thought about growing old before. But these past few weeks had him wondering how much longer his body would be able to take the punishment of rodeoing.

He didn't have a plan B. At twenty-nine, he'd never slowed down enough to consider anything but the next event or the next town. Slowing down gave a man way too much time to think. Dallas needed action to keep his life on an even keel.

"Gonna try Maggie's?" Wilson asked.

"I guess." Dallas supposed coffee and a cinnamon apple twist without the conversation was better than nothing.

"Say hey to your dad for me." Wilson's voice followed Dallas as he headed back to his truck.

"Will do. See you."

"See you," Wilson echoed.

Dallas drove the block to Maggie's and pulled in up front. The open sign was lit up above blue checkerboard half curtains covering the lower half of the front windows. Two hanging baskets of flowers bracketed the glass door, which stood open.

From across the sidewalk, Dallas could smell the yeast and sugar.

The buzz of cheerful voices also wafted through the doorway as he crossed the sidewalk. Conversations were layered on top of each other, signaling a lively mostly female crowd in the midafternoon.

"It's way too early to tell, truly." The unexpected sound of Sierra's voice stopped him in his tracks.

"It reminds me of that girl… What was her name?" McKinney answered back, surprising him even more. "The one with the rainbow hair."

"That describes more than one woman on campus." There was a thread of laughter in Sierra's voice.

"In Botany 101. She rode that low bike. Kind of unusual."

"Recumbent. I remember."

Dallas scrambled to make sense of the conversation. McKinney and Sierra knew each other from college?

"Like *that*." There was a triumphant ring to McKinney's voice.

"I'm not seeing it," Sierra said.

"It all went bad during our lab that time."

"Ohhhh," Sierra said. "I hadn't thought of it from that—"

Dallas stepped inside.

"—angle." Sierra continued talking, her back to him. "But, I'll—"

"Hello, Dallas." The warning tone and the look in McKinney's eyes betrayed both surprise and guilt.

Sierra stopped talking.

He stepped up to their window table, taking a wide stance.

Sierra nervously moistened her lips, then offered him a smile.

It turned him on—annoyingly.

Fighting the feeling, he furrowed his brow and glanced back and forth between them. "And you two are…?" He waited for an explanation.

"Having doughnuts," McKinney said, pointing to her vanilla glazed.

"They're delicious," Sierra said. A custard cream sat on her plate.

He waited a moment longer, but neither of them offered more. It was obvious they didn't know how much he'd overheard.

He decided to get the ball rolling himself. "You were in college together?"

Oddly, they both looked relieved.

He hadn't expected that.

"Oh, that," McKinney said.

"We had some classes in common," Sierra added.

"So, you knew each other. Way back then." He didn't know what was up here, but something was definitely going on. Otherwise, they'd have mentioned their friendship before now.

The two women exchanged a glance.

"Sure," McKinney told him.

"So, you lied."

"About what?" she asked, feigning innocence.

"About there being an equal opportunity initiative." At least one thing made more sense to him now—why McKinney tried to give Sierra a guest room instead of putting her in staff quarters.

Sierra looked distinctly uncomfortable, adjusting herself in the parlor chair.

McKinney looked affronted.

But Dallas wasn't buying her offense.

"Why?" he asked, hoping to shake lose some more information.

"We didn't lie," McKinney said. "I've been working on an equal opportunity initiative for months now. Sierra just happens to be the first candidate."

"The completely unsuitable woman you knew in college."

"Yes." McKinney looked him straight in the eye, daring him to argue.

Dallas switched to Sierra to see if she was any easier to read.

"Dallas," McKinney said in a low voice—an obvious ploy to throw him off the scent.

He ignored her, fixating on Sierra instead. But something shifted, and he lost track of his thought process. He couldn't keep focus, couldn't ignore the memories of their passionate kiss and the feel of her in his arms.

"Dallas," McKinney repeated more harshly.

Sierra's gaze was steady, warm and deep. The blue of her irises softened. He felt their drag along with an odd hitch in his chest.

"We're attracting attention," McKinney hissed in an undertone.

Sierra suddenly blinked and pulled back a fraction of an inch. She cleared her throat and shifted once more in her seat.

"Would you like to sit down?" she asked Dallas.

"No." He didn't want to sit down.

He didn't want to sit down and make small talk. He didn't want to feel this way about her. And he sure wanted some answers.

He couldn't get them right now—not here in front of neighbors and strangers. And not with Sierra distracting him.

He wondered then if it was on purpose. Was she using her bedroom eyes and that flirty, pouty expression to make him forget what he was doing?

"I'll take mine to go," he said flatly.

"You don't need to be angry," McKinney said.

"I'm not angry." *Angry* wasn't the right word.

Confounded was a better one. He was confounded by a lot of things right now—his family, his future and even more by his reaction to Sierra.

Needing to clear her head and banish her unsettling feelings for Dallas, Sierra paced the cobblestone pathway that circled the sprawling Hawkes mansion. It was late evening. Dinner was over, and she'd helped a cheerful group of staff members get the kitchen ready for the morning.

The cool air felt good on her face. The wind was light, puffing with the fragrance of sweetgrass and ponderosa pine. The moon was a mere sliver of white light hanging over the western horizon, while the sky was awash in the pinpoints of stars.

Though it was lovely here in the mountains, she missed the salt tang of the ocean and the rhythmic sound of the waves. She might have left Carmel under a cloud, but she'd also left fond memories—growing up with her mom and their friends, even time spent with her dad before he'd left.

She missed Nancy and made a mental note to check in with her friend in LA. Nancy was a comforting touchstone now that Sierra's life had taken such an unexpected turn.

She thought about Roger for the first time in days, letting herself probe the relationship, assigning most of the blame to him, but some of it to herself as well. She'd been foolish to let him become her whole life.

After turning to go back, she paused on the footbridge over the brook, listening to the low sound of the burbling waterfall. She vowed to turn these past weeks into life lessons and use them moving forward. She'd find her own path from now on, her own passions, her very own destiny in life.

She turned her mind to happier Carmel thoughts, to

Chardonnay with Nancy on the balcony, volleyball on the beach and lattes at High Brew the sidewalk café on Bramble Street. Their coffee had been smooth and sweet, their scones tender and the clotted cream and locally made jam a feast for the senses. Her smile faded a little as she missed Nancy even more.

She'd call her later tonight and explain the past two weeks. She could only imagine Nancy's surprise at learning the engagement was off, never mind that Sierra was in Colorado on a cattle ranch.

Sierra sighed and closed her eyes, reaching for the railing to anchor herself. She was going to do what she advised her clients. She'd go on from here with the stronger emotional foundation.

Dallas tried to crowd his way into her psyche, but she pushed back on the image. Someday she'd be able to appreciate his good looks without the emotional baggage. But not just yet.

She blinked open her eyes and focused on the pond. It shimmered with light from the waterfall frothing at the far end of the bridge. She inhaled the fresh scents, struggling to center herself.

When Dallas's image refused to leave, she started walking, following the softly glowing lamps on the stone walls and the pot lights shining up from the gardens.

She saw the heat in his deep dark eyes. Back there in the bakery, a sizzling undercurrent had arced between them—as if five seconds had passed instead of five days since they'd kissed.

Those same feelings welled up now, bringing the glow of excitement, the thrill of arousal, tasting his essence, waiting and hoping he'd pull her closer, kiss her deeper, and—

"Your head's sure up there in the clouds." Mrs. Innish

startled Sierra to a stop as she spoke from a bench outside the kitchen door.

The older woman was in shadows, a cigarette tip glowing bright orange in her hand.

A curl of tobacco smoke invaded Sierra's nostrils, and she wrinkled them, resisting an urge to fan the air in front of her. She hadn't known Mrs. Innish was a smoker.

She curbed the compulsion to warn the woman about the health risks of smoking. She'd had that particular conversation with more than a few of her clients—in fact, far too many for her peace of mind.

"Want one?" Mrs. Innish held out the pack.

"No thanks." It was the most polite thing Sierra could think of to say.

"Don't smoke?"

Sierra bit her tongue and shook her head—lung cancer, stroke, cardiovascular disease, never mind early menopause and skin damage, to name just a few of the dangers of the tar and toxic chemicals that laced the tobacco.

"Thinking of quitting myself," Mrs. Innish said, frowning at her half-smoked cigarette.

"Good for you." Sierra tried to sound encouraging without coming across as judgmental.

"Tough to do. I'm down to five a day."

"That sounds like solid progress." Sierra sat down on the opposite end of the bench, feeling it her duty to help. "Have you tried nicotine gum? Hypnosis?"

Mrs. Innish stubbed out her cigarette. *"Hypnosis?"*

"Some people find it works." Sierra knew a couple of psychologists who used hypnosis to combat a whole host of habits and addictions.

"Don't much go in for that theatrical stuff."

Sierra fought a smile at that. "I meant a licensed clinician, not at a carnival or anything."

To her surprise, Mrs. Innish smiled back, a joking tone to her voice. "I'll admit I *was* picturing a tattered old woman with tarot cards and a crystal ball."

Sierra was taken aback. She would have bet Mrs. Innish didn't have a sense of humor.

"It's nothing like that," Sierra said.

"Probably I'd have to go to Denver or something."

Sierra suspected that was true. "I could get a recommendation for you."

Mrs. Innish looked puzzled.

"I worked at a wellness center in Carmel."

"Ah. California."

"Yes, California."

"And what does someone do at a wellness center in California?"

Sierra skirted around her real role. "We offered yoga and dietary advice. I also sold natural lotions and teas. Botanical treatments can be quite effective. Black pepper and angelica oil, for example, can relieve the craving for nicotine."

Mrs. Innish raised her brows, her astonishment clear. "You went from *that* to ranching?"

Dallas's voice joined the conversation as his boots scraped against the concrete. "That's a really good question." He stepped up and zeroed in on Sierra. "It seems like a stretch."

"I'm a trainee ranch hand," Sierra answered staunchly. She didn't know how much he'd overheard, but she knew she hadn't said anything that would give away her true mission.

"Hello, Dallas." Mrs. Innish greeted him respectfully.

Dallas gave her a nod in return. "Evening, Bea." Then he looked back at Sierra, cocking his head quizzically. "I don't see the connection."

The connection might not be obvious, but Sierra had given her answer some thought. "What are grass and oats if not botanicals?"

"Forage," he responded dryly.

"Same thing." Sierra counted off on her fingers, glad to finally find herself in her comfort zone. "Carbohydrates, protein, lipids, cellulose, minerals and fatty acids."

"You're telling me you're interested in livestock nutrition?"

"Who isn't?"

"Somewhere north of ninety-nine percent of the population. And I'm guessing that figure's higher in Carmel, California."

Mrs. Innish pushed to her feet. "I think I'll leave you youngsters to it."

"Night," Dallas said to her.

"Good night," Sierra echoed.

As Mrs. Innish gave them a wave and went on her way, Sierra made a mental note to track down some black pepper and angelica oil and at least make her the offer of help.

"I didn't think you two got along," Dallas said as the back door clicked shut.

"She surprised me," Sierra answered, not sure now how to frame her overall opinion of Mrs. Innish.

"How?"

"She cracked a joke."

Dallas's speculative gaze retraced Mrs. Innish's path to the door. "Really?"

"Yes."

"Are you sure?"

"I'm positive. She compared hypnosis to reading a crystal ball."

Dallas relaxed his stance. "How is that a joke?"

"Well, one has empirical evidence. The other is a con game used to fleece carnival-goers."

"Which is which?"

"Ha, ha."

Dallas raised his brows, looking serious.

"You can't mean that." She paused, but he didn't respond. "There is zero evidence for fortune-telling. But there are dozens of peer-reviewed case studies of hypnosis. People lose weight, stop smoking. It reduces pain, depression, anxiety."

"Power of suggestion," he said.

"Well, duh. That's exactly what it is." Sierra considered the brain the most powerful organ in the human body.

"The power of suggestion is hardly lab-tested."

"Something doesn't have to be lab-tested to work."

"It helps." Dallas chuckled.

"It's in your brain," Sierra countered, leaning forward and gesturing to his temple to make her point. "Hypnosis is used to cope with anxiety and pain. Like meditating, it can increase endorphins That's the science."

"It only works if you think it's going to work."

"Who cares why it works?"

He took a half step, closing the distance between them, the lights behind the waterfall shifting over the planes of his face. "A temporary placebo effect isn't the same as a cure."

"If it makes you quit smoking, it's a cure."

He seemed amused. "Do you know how hard it is to follow your logic?"

She tapped once on his chest. "Do you know how hard it is to penetrate your stubbornness?"

"I imagine it's tough."

"You imagine right."

"Why are you trying?"

She drew back a few inches, acknowledging it was a good question—at least from his perspective. It took her a moment to form an answer. "I feel like you can be redeemed."

Dallas's lips split into a grin.

His humor was infectious, and she returned the smile.

"You'd be wrong on that," he said.

"I don't think so." It was their first meaningful conversation about his feelings, and she wondered how far she dared push. She was hesitant, but she knew she had to try.

She gestured to his injured shoulder. "Who knows, maybe it can help you."

He instantly sobered, and she knew she'd misplayed her hand.

"You think this is all in my head?"

"That's not what I meant."

He took a step back, his eyes narrowing. "A sugar pill or a dangling pocket watch, and I'll be just fine? Is that what you think?"

She scrambled to recover. "No, Dallas, honestly—"

"Good night, Sierra." He pivoted.

She opened her mouth to call out, but she knew she'd blown her chance.

She had to let him go, regroup, then try again, unfortunately, from an even weaker position.

Six

A man needed to work hard. He needed to throw himself into physical activity to keep his mind quiet, his emotions at bay and to sleep soundly through the night.

Dallas had tried to do that today.

Despite rejecting Sierra's theories of what amounted to mind over matter, he was desperate enough to give anything a shot. He'd done a little quasi-meditation this morning, trying hard to get into the zone—whatever that was. He'd heard about it once from a woman he'd met in a bar in Mesquite.

He was skeptical, but if his body truly was capable of manufacturing natural painkillers, it could only help with the healing process. And he had to admit, he liked the idea of engaging every scrap of healing power in his own body.

Afterward, he took some ibuprofen because he was still a diehard fan of lab-tested remedies. Then he forcibly shoved the pain to the back of his mind and set out with some of the other cowboys to mend fence.

Despite his best mental efforts, the pain had grown worse each passing hour. Now he could barely lift his arm.

It was just him and his dad at the dinner table tonight. Luckily, Victor had served beef stew and fresh rolls, and Dallas's father didn't seem to notice his struggle to eat one-handed as they each focused on their own meal.

"You went out with the fence crew today," his dad opened, several mouthfuls in.

"I did." Dallas didn't expect a thank-you or any praise for that, more likely he'd get a query about the fence and range conditions.

"Why?" The question was curt and demanding.

Dallas stopped eating and glanced at his father's glowering expression. "Because the fences needed mending," he answered flatly.

"We have people to do that."

"I know we do. I'm one of them."

"You're not."

"What's that supposed to mean?" Dallas would pull his weight to the very best of his ability.

His father made a gesture with his empty fork. "It means you're a rancher, not a cowboy."

"You're a rancher," Dallas countered. "I'm a cowboy."

His father's jaw clenched. "Son—"

Dallas didn't like where the conversation was going. "I'll help while I'm here. But let's not pretend this is permanent." He'd made his choice to leave years ago. His father and everyone else knew why.

His father's chest heaved. "You *belong* with the family."

Dallas took a deep breath, his shoulder throbbing more insistently. They'd had this conversation backward, forward and sideways, many times over. Memories of his mother's death were magnified for Dallas in a way the rest of his family didn't seem to understand.

"My life. My choice," he answered back.

"Will you get realistic." Garrett gestured to Dallas's shoulder. "Rodeoing is too dangerous."

"And cowboying is so much safer?"

"Yes! Yes. Many, many times over. And it has a future. Our future for generations to come."

There it was. Dallas was still hungry, but he pushed back from the table. "We're not doing this."

"Oh, yes we are," his father thundered.

"You have Austin. You have Tyler. You have McKinney. Why do you fixate on me?"

"You all need to pull your weight."

"You mean settle in and give you grandchildren."

"You know it's far more than that."

Dallas rose. "What I know is that it's *your* dream, not mine."

"It's not a dream. It's a legacy. It's a duty. You know how close we came to losing it."

"And why is that? Why, Dad? Could it be because it was *dangerous*?"

His father's nostrils flared and a ruddy flush rose on his lined face.

Dallas wished he could take back the words. He'd gone too far this time. His father had been left alone to run the ranch because his only sibling had died as a young man, trampled during a cattle drive.

But Dallas couldn't make up for the past. And he wasn't going to try.

"I'm going back." He shifted his chair out of the way. "Just as soon as I'm healed, I am going back."

"You have responsibilities here and now."

"To myself. Not to you."

His father's stare turned icy. "To your family, your grandfather and the generations before him."

Dallas clamped his jaw. The ranch had been in the Hawkes family for six generations, and his father envisioned it lasting for many more.

"I have two brothers," Dallas said. He also had a sister who seemed to love ranching. The place was in good hands no matter what Dallas did.

"Tyler is overseas."

"He's coming home." Dallas refused to believe his younger brother would be harmed in his military service. He wasn't in a war zone. "He's a good cowboy."

"It's a big ranch."

"You ran it yourself."

Some of the anger went out of Garrett's voice. "It nearly killed me."

Dallas knew it was an exaggeration. Eighty-thousand acres was a lot for one man to manage. But his father was born and bred to it, and Dallas had been on the receiving end of his father's emotional manipulation for years. Garrett would use anything to keep Dallas in line.

"Define *nearly*," Dallas challenged softly.

Garrett tossed his napkin down on the table like a gauntlet and rose to his feet. He was the same height as Dallas, and the two men stared at each other.

"Can we once, just once, have a civilized conversation?"

"Not about this."

Garrett's nostrils flared. He shook his head in apparent disgust. After a moment, he turned away.

As he watched his father pace stiffly up the staircase, Dallas wished he'd been the one to leave. It was a power move—also emblematic.

He gripped the back of his chair in frustration, then cussed as a sharp shaft of pain ricocheted through his shoulder.

Sierra had been wrong.

It was adrenaline and grit that had kept him going today. Endorphins had nothing to do with it.

He stepped away from the table. At this point, a double shot of whiskey was going to do more for him than lukewarm beef stew.

In the corner sitting room off the front hall, he flipped on the gas fireplace. At the wet bar, he poured a measure of dark, amber-hued aged barrel oak whiskey into a heavy tumbler and took a swig, letting the sweet, smoky flavor warm his throat as he settled himself in a leather armchair. He faced his sore shoulder to the flames and took another drink.

He closed his eyes and flexed, grimacing and hoping desperately he hadn't set his recovery back too far today.

"You look like you're in pain." It was Sierra's soft voice in the doorway behind him.

"Go away," he told her without looking. He wasn't fit to talk to anyone right now, let alone her.

Her footsteps drew closer. "Maybe I can—"

"I said, *go away*."

"Do you have a prescription?" she asked, seemingly unperturbed by his outburst.

"Yes."

"Do you need a pill?"

He could hear that she was standing right above him now.

"I don't need a nurse."

She drew a sigh. "You need something, Dallas."

He didn't like the way his name sounded on her lips. Scratch that. He loved the way his name sounded on her lips. But he wasn't in the mood for anything to make him feel better right now. He wanted to sit here and wallow in his misery.

She touched his shoulder.

He flinched away, his eyes opening wide.

"Don't," he rasped.

"I'll be gentle." She rested her fingertips there.

Her hands were warm and light. They didn't hurt at all.

"Oh, wow," she said, sliding the tips of her fingers along the contour of his shoulder, making her way to the cords of his neck. "You feel like a concrete block."

"Thanks," he said sarcastically.

She slowly worked her way back to the tip of his shoulder, pressing a little harder along the way.

It hurt this time, but it wasn't a bad hurt.

She paused on a spot above his clavicle and made a circle with the pad of her thumb.

He groaned.

"You need to loosen up," she said, widening the circle, adding her fingers and her other thumb to the mix.

He wanted to tell her to stop. He wanted to repeat his demand that she butt out of his life. But her touch was so warm and comforting. She pressed gently into the muscles around his injury, sending tingles along his arm, down his back and up his neck.

He didn't mind that kind of pain. It told him she was hitting the right spots.

"Relax," she urged him in a soft, vibrating voice. "Nothing matters right now. Let your body do its work."

He was exhausted both mentally and physically. Instead of demanding she stop, he closed his eyes and banished his worries. He focused on the faint hiss of the warm fire, breathed in her sweet scent and let her talented hands dig into the knotted fibers of his shoulder.

Sierra had seen a second chance to connect with Dallas, and she'd taken it.

He wasn't complaining, but she knew she had to be

hurting him with the massage. His muscles were tangled up in stiff knots from protecting his injury, and the only way to encourage them to release their death grip was to increase the pressure. He needed better blood flow, and he needed it now.

The air was warm, the lighting low, and the firelight flicked pale orange against the caramel-colored sofa and polished wood tables. It was a lovely little room, comfortable, with a sofa and armchairs that looked well used, telling her family members must spend a lot of time in here. She thought she would too if she was them.

Dallas flinched.

"Tell me if I hurt you," she said.

"It's fine," he answered on a hiss that told her it wasn't fine at all.

"It'll help, I promise."

"It's helping."

"Good." She wished she dared ask him to remove his shirt. She also wished she had some oil with her, jojoba or arnica, or her personal go-to blend of sweet almond, lavender, marjoram and peppermint.

He flinched again and sucked in a tight breath.

She moved farther along his shoulder, away from a trigger point and closer to his neck, lengthening her strokes to untangle the muscle fibers.

He was in excellent shape. His deltoids and trapezoids were developed and well defined. It didn't surprise her. Rodeo was a highly physical sport. And, according to McKinney, Dallas had spent his formative years as a hardworking cowboy.

"You could get paid for this," Dallas muttered.

She couldn't help but smile. "Paid to torture people?"

"It's not torture."

She dug in a little deeper.

He gasped again. "Hey."

"It's good for you," she assured him. "The tension in your muscles is restricting blood flow to your tendons. Your body can't heal if it's a block of concrete."

"I tried for endorphins today."

His words surprised her.

"How did that go?" she asked.

"Didn't work at all."

That was disappointing to hear. "You might need the help of a professional."

"I don't see that happening."

She moved down the inside of his shoulder blade, searching for supple muscle so she could work her way back toward the injury. "You're stubborn as a mule."

"Me? *Me?* You're the one who won't admit she has no business working on a ranch."

"I'm broadening my horizons."

"There are a thousand ways to broaden your horizons."

"Maybe." She'd admit he was right about that. "But I've picked this one."

"Why?"

"Why not?"

"That's not an answer."

She stroked her fingertips upward, hitting tense muscle again, making little vibrating circles deep into the tissue.

He flinched and hissed. "Is this your revenge?"

"Not at all. It's bribery."

"You mean extortion."

"No. I mean bribery. I figure if I make you feel better, you'll stop pushing to have me fired."

It was a moment before he spoke. "Where did you hear that?"

She didn't want to admit to eavesdropping, so she answered dramatically. "The walls have ears."

He turned, forcing her to stop massaging. "No, seriously. How did you know that? Did McKinney tell you?"

Sierra regretted her honesty. "No. She didn't. Now turn." She gently guided him, and he surprised her by complying.

"You're not going to tell me, are you?"

She tried for a joke. "I'm protecting the innocent."

"Fine. But my other question stands."

"What question is that?"

"Why are you so insistent on staying?"

Sierra decided it was time for the truth—at least part of the truth.

"I'll make you a deal," she said.

He tipped his head to peer up at her.

"You take off your shirt."

His eyes darkened, and she realized how it had sounded.

"For the massage," she clarified. "You take off your shirt so I can do a better job massaging you, and I'll tell you why I want to stay."

He hesitated for a moment, looking like he was trying to read her mind. "This better be good."

"Don't tell me you're shy," she teased.

His gaze warmed to smoldering, its intensity causing a flutter in her chest, making her rethink the request for a fraction of a second before she reminded herself that she worked on unclothed bodies all the time. This was professional, not personal.

She regrouped. "It'll let me do a much better job."

"Okay." His voice was intimately low as he reached for the buttons on his shirt.

She held her breath as he popped them one by one.

Though she fought it hard, her mind took off in all kinds of sensual directions.

His smooth chest was revealed first, the curve of his

pecs and the indentation between, then his washboard abs, then the shirt slipped from his shoulders, over his biceps and down to his wrists.

Desire pooled in Sierra's stomach. Image after image of Dallas flooded her mind, filling up her memory.

He tossed the shirt onto the low table in front of them and leaned forward in the chair to give her better access.

She took a bracing breath before putting her hands on his bare shoulder.

His skin was warm to her touch, smooth and slick. His deltoid looked like the perfect spot to place a kiss—his shoulder, then his neck, then his lips.

Heat flowed through her, and she trembled a little bit.

She ordered herself to focus on his injury. She moved her thumbs to the base of his rhomboids and circled them upward. It was smooth going at first, but tension increased as she worked her way toward his left shoulder.

"Start talking," he said.

"I broke up with my fiancé," she said, letting her hands go on autopilot. "I mean, he broke up with me. It came as a shock. Well, somewhat of a shock, I guess."

When the spark dimmed between her and Roger, she hadn't wanted to admit it. She was grateful now that he had.

"What happened?" Dallas asked.

"He found someone else."

Dallas twisted his head to look back. "Seriously?"

His incredulity warmed her heart.

"Thanks for that," she said. "Diva was far more glamorous than I'll ever be."

"Diva?"

"Her real name was Devin. But she had this attitude—a perfectionist when it came to her looks and an opinion. about, well, everything." Sierra wondered if that had been the attraction for Roger—that Devin was so different from him, so different from Sierra too.

"Not in a good way?" Dallas guessed.

"Her flare for makeup and fashion was quite dramatic, but men sure seemed to like it. You'd probably like it."

"I doubt it."

Sierra didn't argue, but she guessed beauty like Diva's was pretty much universal. "She had thick blond hair with shimmering highlights and curves in all the right places. She wore pretty fabrics with flowing lines and lace here and there. And her shoes. Wow. She had some shoe collection."

"I'm not a shoe guy."

She thought back to her own small collection. "I've bought a few pairs over the years. I can appreciate a nice set of spike heels."

Dallas glanced at her feet. At the moment, they were wrapped in denim blue slip-on walking shoes.

"Not these," she said, turning her bare ankle.

"I have an imagination. Did you bring any of them to the ranch?" There was a hopeful note to his voice.

"Are you mocking me?"

"No."

She couldn't tell if he was being serious. "Are you a shoe guy?"

He paused. "Maybe."

She detected a smirk in his voice, so she answered tartly. "I left them behind."

He sighed theatrically. "Too bad."

"I can't tell if you're joking or not."

"Joking about what?"

"Liking shoes."

"Most guys like shoes. Nice ones. On women. We don't care about our own."

It was her turn to make a joke since she'd seen his worn cowboy boots. "Shock, that."

He chuckled, then he tensed from the pain.

"You have to relax," she reminded him.

"Maybe you could get them shipped here?" he suggested.

"Not going to happen." The shoes and everything else were lost to her now.

"Why not?"

"I left in a hurry." That sounded bad, like she was guilty, fleeing a crime or something. "Not in hurry, hurry. But I didn't much feel like packing up my stuff."

"Because?" It was clear Dallas was confused.

Sierra hadn't wanted to go into this much detail, but it was hard to avoid at this point. "Because it was Roger's condo. It was Roger's business. It was pretty much Roger's life."

"You worked for the guy too?" Dallas asked.

She realized they'd wandered a little too close to the whole truth. She needed to get creative here. She repeated the story she'd given Mrs. Innish. "Opuntia Lifestyles. We sold natural products, botanicals, lotions, lifestyle improvement."

"So, he was a huckster."

Sierra rose to Opuntia Lifestyles' defense. "That's not a fair characterization."

"You don't have to defend him."

"I'm not defending *him*. I told you, natural remedies are very effective."

"I'm still a firm believer in pharmacology and medical science."

"And what would you call this?" She increased the pressure in her fingers.

He groaned.

She backed off. "Sorry."

"No. It's good. It hurts good."

She put the pressure back on. "Massage is a natural remedy."

"Backed by science."

"Sure. You want to understand anatomy to do it right. But it uses no drugs, no surgical intervention."

Dallas went silent for a moment, and she felt as though she'd made her point.

"When did he start dating Diva?" Dallas asked into the silence.

"I don't know." Sierra tried to stay dispassionate as she thought her way through the question. "But I guess I should have seen it coming. Devin lit a room. She lit up men. She lit up Roger."

"You sound jealous."

Sierra stilled. Her tone turned clipped. "I'm not."

"You sure?"

She let her hands slide from his shoulder and stepped back, surprised that's what he'd taken from their conversation. "Absolutely."

He straightened in the chair and took in her expression. "You might want to give your answer some serious thought."

She'd given it all the serious thought it needed. And it was time to cut this conversation short before she alienated him all over again.

But his gaze darkened in the silence, impatience coming through in his tone. "We're not a rehab facility for the lovelorn, you know."

She summoned all her professionalism to keep her voice even. "I never thought you were. Good night, Dallas."

Seven

Dallas spent a full day telling himself he was right. Then he spent the next two days admitting he was wrong.

He'd been thrown off-balance by the thought of Sierra pining away for another man. But she could be as jealous as she wanted of her ex's new girlfriend. And she was perfectly free to use the Hawkes ranch as a rehab facility for the lovelorn while she did her job. In either case, it was none of his business.

What he should have said was thank you. He should have kept his mouth shut about her personal life and told her how much he appreciated the massage that had his shoulder feeling better than it had since the accident.

Against that backdrop of regret, he was a reluctant attendee in Jagged Creek tonight, walking the opulent ballroom of the Oberfeld Hotel. But at least his walk was easy. His shoulder was loose. For the first time since his injury, it felt like the true healing had begun.

The Hawkes ranch crew had arrived as a group in several ranch vehicles. Now, he looked around for Sierra, intending to offer the overdue apology and thank her the way she deserved. But he couldn't find her in the crowd.

Hundreds of finely dressed ranchers and residents chatted their way around the cavernous room. It was elaborately decorated, with muted lighting and high ceilings draped in miles of backlit purple-and-white tulle. Faux candles flickered inside lavender rose centerpieces perched on the high, white tables around the perimeter of the dance floor.

The event was billed as a thank-you to the townspeople of Jagged Creek, a pre-opening gala so the locals could get a look inside the new place. Dallas had done a double take walking past the white-light-decorated palm trees that lined the entryway. It was an odd choice for northwestern Colorado.

Waitstaff wandered through the crowd carrying silver trays that offered a wide selection of little hors d'oeuvres. But they were fussy and fiddly. Some had curls of greens or sprinklings of nuts and seeds. He saw a mini shrimp salad in a shot glass—one lonely shrimp on what looked like a bed of clover.

Dallas opted for a beer, ending up with something dark and hoppy imported from Germany. Then he spotted Sierra across the room, and his mood lifted.

Earlier, he'd caught a flash of her blue dress as she climbed into one of the trucks leaving the ranch. He took a better look now, seeing it had a soft, two-layered skirt that fell to her midthigh, revealing her beautiful legs. He could have stared at them all night. But the rest of her deserved attention too.

Her shoulders were bare and smooth. Flat lace highlighted a scooped halter neck above the clinging fabric that outlined her breasts and waist before flaring out into the silky-soft skirt.

He didn't know where she'd found the shoes, but they were off-the-charts sexy—silver and midnight blue, high and strappy, with open toes and a sexy ankle band that gave a jolt to his nervous system. He couldn't help but admire what they did to her calves as he moved closer for a better look.

As he wound his way through the crowd and the high tables, music came up from the live band set up in one corner. The opening bars of a country tune were rich and skillfully played. Dallas couldn't help but admire the talent of their lead guitar.

A cowboy Dallas didn't recognize walked up to Sierra, blocking his view. Dallas quickened his steps.

She smiled at the man, laughed easily, then nodded her head yes.

The cowboy offered his hand. She took it, looking relaxed and cheerful as she followed the man onto the dance floor to join the dozens of couples taking advantage of the lively music.

Dallas wished he'd thought of it first, made his move earlier and got her out on the dance floor, where they could talk. He positioned himself close by, making up his mind to be next.

He recognized the final chorus of the song and started toward her.

He caught sight of another cowboy doing the same thing. He recognized the new guy as being from the Circle Seth, although he didn't know his name.

"Dance?" Dallas asked Sierra before she even stopped moving.

"Dance?" the Circle Seth guy echoed, shooting Dallas a hard look as he held out his hand.

Sierra seemed taken aback as she looked from one to the other.

"Okay," she said to Dallas as she stepped out of the first cowboy's arms.

The cowboy looked disappointed.

She offered a polite smile and a helpless shrug to the Circle Seth guy. "Sorry."

The guy didn't move.

Dallas sent him a glare. He got a level gaze of defiance in return.

"I'll take the next one," Circle Seth said to Sierra.

Dallas bristled at the assumption. "That's up to her."

"I'm tapping out," the first cowboy said with good humor as he turned away.

Dallas didn't wait for any more discussion. The music started up again, a slower song this time. He took Sierra in his arms, keeping a few respectful inches between them.

"Were you looking for a dance or a showdown?" she asked as they settled into the rhythm of the music.

He wondered if she meant with the Circle Seth guy or with her. He'd guess her, given how their last encounter had ended. Plus, she'd obviously made a point of staying out of his way the past few days.

But he feigned confusion. "What do you mean?"

She canted her head toward the Circle Seth guy walking away. "You looked like you wanted to fight."

The answer surprised Dallas, but he gratefully rolled with it. "No showdown necessary."

"Are you saying you won't fight for me?" She was teasing now.

"Who do you want me to fight?"

"Nobody."

"Okay."

Since she didn't seem angry with him, he took a chance

and settled her a little more closely in his arms. She was lithe and light, easily following his lead, dancing smoothly as they made their way around the floor. He knew he still owed her an apology. And he was warming up to it. But he didn't want to mess with this moment.

They danced silently through the opening verse, a sense of warmth and well-being making its way through him.

"Did McKinney send you over?" Sierra asked.

"To apologize?" He wasn't surprised Sierra had told his sister about his rudeness.

Sierra seemed amused by his answer. "To ask me to dance."

"Why would she want us to dance?"

There was a split second of silence. "To make sure I didn't feel neglected. I don't really know anyone here."

"You got plenty of guys stepping up as partners." Dallas dared to firm his hand in the small of Sierra's back, feeling oddly possessive when he thought about the other cowboys.

She didn't exactly melt against him, but their bodies brushed together, her heat teasing his senses.

He drew a breath and forced himself to speak. "I know I owe you an apology."

"It's fine," she said, not bothering to pretend she didn't know what he meant.

"No. It's not fine. Your personal life is none of my business."

It took her a moment to respond. "I told you freely."

"But I shouldn't have offered an opinion. You're McKinney's guest. And you were graciously helping me. I should have been more respectful."

Recognizing the halfway mark in the popular song, Dallas felt an odd sense of panic at the thought of letting her go.

She looked up then, her beautiful bright eyes touching

something deep inside him. "Thanks for that. Also, thanks for helping me learn the ropes."

"I haven't done a thing." He was embarrassed by that now. He'd been stubborn and short with her along with everyone else.

"You helped with Cedric."

"I mocked you with Cedric." What he remembered most vividly was that he'd kissed her with Cedric.

He gave in to the urge to move closer still. He splayed his fingers out across her back and drew their joined hands closer to their bodies.

She didn't resist. "How are you feeling now? Your shoulder?"

"Your massage helped." The dance was helping too somehow. His world had slowed down with her in his arms, his pain untangling as pleasure crowded it out.

"I knew it would." There was a smile in her voice.

"Is that an I-told-you-so?"

"It was."

"Don't sound so smug." He couldn't resist teasing her back. "It's not like you massaged me with your crystal ball."

"I don't have a crystal ball. But I do have some trigger-point massage balls."

"That's still science."

She was silent for a moment. "You shouldn't discount everything you can't see and feel. Thoughts and emotions are very powerful."

He wouldn't argue that since he was having some pretty powerful thoughts and emotions right now. One of them was to kiss her, starting with her lips, her neck, the tip of her shoulder.

The song was winding down, and he dreaded the end of their dance.

He glanced around for the Circle Seth cowboy, planning to avoid the man and score another dance with Sierra.

Instead, he spotted an open bank of doors leading to the patio.

"Fresh air?" he asked, circling his arm around her waist, and gently urging her toward the doors before she had a chance to answer.

The clear, cool night enveloped Sierra as she walked onto the hotel patio, a soft breeze lifting loose strands from her upswept hair. A new moon rose on the horizon, and the stars were scattered brightly in the dome of the sky. Water burbled past in a shallow bend of the creek that bordered one edge of the dimly lit flagstone patio.

They walked in silence toward a stretch of lawn that fanned out in a V, ending in a lighted line of maple trees. They passed groupings of padded chairs around three flaming gas fireplaces and left the noise of the band and the party behind.

Dallas's arm on her waist lent an intimacy to the situation, and she knew a perfect opportunity when she saw one.

"Enjoying the party?" She opened with something simple, safe, innocuous.

"I am now." His tone was low and sexy, and rumbled against the stone wall beside them.

"You weren't before?" she asked as they made their way farther along the patio and into the shadows.

"Not my thing."

"The crowds?" she asked, not exactly surprised by that. He'd struck her as a loner from the moment she met him—independent and fiercely self-reliant.

"The foofaraw."

"Foofaraw?" She smiled over his choice of words.

"Glittery palm trees, all those hothouse flowers, purple draping and shrimp in a shot glass. Who puts shrimp in a shot glass?"

"Caterers?"

He slowed to stop and turned to face her. "People with too many shot glasses and not enough shrimp, that's who."

"They did taste good."

"Spoken like a Californian."

"Are you picking on my home state?"

"They wouldn't come anywhere near to filling up a Coloradan."

"I don't think that's the point of hors d'oeuvres."

"It's the point of food, isn't it?"

She refocused her questions. "I take it you like your food filling?"

"Don't you?"

"I like it tasty." She didn't want to make this about her. "Favorites?" She lobbed the question back his way.

"Doesn't matter."

"How can it not matter?"

"You put food in front of a hungry cowboy and they either like it or they love it."

She couldn't help smiling at the straightforward answer. "But not shrimp in a shot glass."

His gaze softened on hers. "Not much point in that, really."

"From a cowboy's perspective." Her voice came out lower and huskier than she'd intended. She tried to swallow it away, ignoring the deepening of her heartbeat and the warm flush coming up on her skin.

"Now you're getting it," he said, shifting a little closer.

She knew she needed to back off, but her feet wouldn't move. She managed a response. "No interest in luxuries and extravagances."

"Except maybe shoes." He gave a secretive half smile and slowly looked down. "And certain pretty dresses."

"Dallas," she managed, trying to make it a warning, but it came out more like a capitulation.

He lifted his gaze to her eyes. "On certain beautiful women."

Sierra tried to breathe, but her chest felt too tight to expand. She was trying desperately to ignore her attraction to him, but it wasn't going anywhere.

He smoothed her cheek with the back of his fingers, then brushed back stray wisps of her hair.

"Beautiful," he said, as he slowly dipped forward.

She realized she wanted this more than anything, so she closed her eyes and inhaled his scent, tipping her head to let his lips brush hers.

The kiss was extraordinarily gentle at first, only a faint buzz. But slowly, deliberately, he deepened it, sending a sizzle through her core.

She stepped into the sensations, bringing her thighs, her stomach and her breasts against his firm strength.

He wrapped his arms around her.

She parted her lips, giving him access, reveling in the desire and passion that brought every inch of her to life.

He groaned her name, his palm slipping down her hips, pressing them intimately together.

Arousal hazed over her senses. She was cocooned by his touch, his taste, his scent.

The distant sounds of the music and chatter faded to nothing while the drumbeat of her pulse pounded inside her ears.

He found the zipper at the back of her dress and drew it down.

She hung on tight, pressing against the heat of his chest.

He stroked her bare back, slipping one hand around to her side, resting beneath her breast.

A woman's high voice intruded. "I doubt he even meant it that way."

Sierra and Dallas jumped apart.

"What else could he mean?" a second woman responded.

Their footfalls brought them steadily closer.

Sierra scrambled with her zipper, but she couldn't reach the tab.

"They're coming," Dallas whispered in her ear.

He swiftly turned her to face the voices and wrapped an arm around her waist, holding the two sides of the dress in place just as the women cleared a curve in the wall and spotted them standing there.

"Oh," one of them said, jerking back and putting her hand dramatically to her chest.

"Didn't mean to startle you," Dallas offered apologetically.

"We didn't see you there," the other woman said.

They looked to be in their midfifties, Sierra guessed. Dressed in designer gowns, with perfectly styled hair and impeccable makeup.

They both peered closely, obviously curious to know what they'd interrupted.

Sierra resisted an urge to smooth her hair. If she looked as disheveled as she felt, they probably guessed what was going on. But trying to fix her appearance would only confirm their suspicions.

A cool gust of wind reminded her of her open dress.

"I hope you're enjoying the party," Sierra said in the most even voice she could muster.

"Very much so," one woman said.

The second gave a nod of agreement.

"I loved the crab canapés," Sierra added. "And those

lemon tarts. Did you try one of the lemon tarts? They melt in your mouth." She knew she was babbling.

"I had the cheesecake," the second woman said, seeming to relax a little bit. "To die for."

"Right?" Sierra asked, putting appreciation into her voice even though she hadn't tasted the cheesecake.

"Well." The first woman looked them both suspiciously up and down. "Good night, then."

"Good night," Dallas said smoothly.

"Bye," Sierra said. She added a finger-wave and a smile. Both of which felt ridiculously forced as the women turned away.

She held her breath as they walked farther along the patio.

"Do me up," she rasped to Dallas as soon as they were out of earshot.

He smoothly zipped her dress.

Sierra took a few steadying breaths. "That was—"

"A kiss," he said, moving to face her.

"That wasn't a kiss." It was more than a kiss. It was way beyond a kiss, and they both knew it.

"What else would you call it?"

She wanted to say a mistake, a colossal mistake as well as a professional conflict of interest and maybe a seismic shift of the world's axis. She'd thrown herself headlong into Dallas's arms and loved every second of it. It was the worst possible thing she could have done.

"We can't do this," she told him.

"We already did."

She scowled. "This isn't funny."

"I know. You're right. We'll do what we did last time— forget it ever happened."

"Right," she staunchly agreed. "That's what we'll do."

But their gazes caught and held. In seconds his mocha-brown eyes were smoldering with desire, and his lips parted again.

"Starting right now," she managed, though she desperately wanted another kiss. A small part of her hoped he'd ignore the statement and pull her into his arms.

But he blinked instead and took a step backward. His chest expanded and his jaw firmed with what looked like resolute determination. "Back to the party, then?"

She forced herself to respond with a quick nod. "Yes. Yes."

Dallas hadn't angled to have Sierra ride home from the party in his pickup. But he sure hadn't objected when it happened. He had McKinney to thank for that when she orchestrated who rode where.

Most of the party guests had stayed to the bitter end, enjoying the music, food and drink. So, everyone made their way to their vehicles together as a nighttime storm rolled in from the west. Lightning flashed above the town, and thunder rumbled as the clouds opened up.

Raindrops scattered across the hood as Sierra maneuvered her way into the passenger side of his pickup, and he firmly shut the door behind her.

It took only seconds for him to make it to the driver's seat, but by then rain was sheeting down the windshield. He slammed his own door and shook the water from his hands.

She peered at the driving rain in the parking lot lights. "Well, *that* was just in time."

"Maybe for you." He raked his fingers dramatically through his wet hair and was rewarded with her smile.

"Sorry about that," she said.

"Better my shirt than your dress." That was for sure.

She glanced down. "It is brand-new."

"Good thing we saved it, then." He gazed at her a moment longer, trying to gauge her level of comfort traveling alone with him after their kiss on the patio.

"You had a nice time?" he asked, leaving the question vague as he considered how to bring up the kiss. He'd rather it didn't just hang in the air between them.

They'd gone their separate ways inside the ballroom, and he'd caught several glimpses of her dancing with other cowboys. He'd wanted to ask her to dance again, but she'd been adamant about forgetting the romantic interlude, so he didn't think she'd welcome the invitation.

"It's been a while since I was out on the town," she said. "You?"

By far, the highlight of the evening had been kissing her, followed closely by their dance. Other than that, it wasn't his idea of a good time. As a designated driver, he didn't even have the option of downing a whiskey or two.

"Like I said, not my first choice of an event."

"You ever wonder why?" She watched his expression while she waited for an answer.

"Nope." He buckled up and touched the start button to bring the engine to life, flipping the windshield wipers to high. He checked the rearview mirror and saw a minor traffic jam behind them.

"Most people like parties," she said.

"I'm not most people." He shut off the wipers, took his foot off the brake and let the truck idle. There was no point in fighting with the crowd just yet.

She glanced out the back window, then took a half turn on the seat so she was facing him. "What do you like in a party?"

He couldn't help thinking about the honky-tonks he and the other cowboys had been to on the road. They'd had some wild and fun nights back then. "Blue jeans, beer in a bottle and peanut shells on the floor."

"Is that the rodeo lifestyle?"

That was part of it to be sure. "Dusty days and rockin' nights."

"I can see why you'd want to rush back to it." There was more than a trace of sarcasm in her voice.

He wasn't going to defend himself. "It can be fun. It's definitely exciting."

"I'm sure it is."

"Judgmental much?" he couldn't help but ask. It seemed clear tonight was more her kind of event and her kind of crowd.

"I didn't mean it to sound like that."

"You showed your true feelings accidentally?"

Their gazes locked and held.

"I'm not a snob," she said.

"I didn't say you were."

"You're entitled to live your own life."

"Thank you." His tone was flat as he glanced in the rearview mirror to see if people had worked themselves out of the gridlock.

They hadn't, and he shook his head at their ineptitude. Clearly, most of them had never done any cattle herding.

"Can I rephrase?" she asked.

"Go for it." He relaxed in the seat, acknowledging they'd be here for a while.

"What draws you to rodeo?"

"It's not here," he said before he had a chance to think it through.

Her brows drew together in confusion. "You mean at a fancy party?"

"I mean in Jagged Creek."

"Really." She seemed to consider his answer. "This part of Colorado seems like cowboy heaven."

He wasn't about to explain his family history, the crushing weight of six generations, and the expectations and the failures that came with being a Hawkes.

"The rodeo ring is cowboy heaven." He watched the vehicles moving steadily toward the exit.

"But if you can't—" She seemed to stop herself.

He knew what she was going to ask. It was on his entire family's mind. He put the truck in Reverse, ready to back from the space.

"Can't what?" He didn't know why he was making her spit it out. He didn't want to have this conversation.

"Compete in the rodeo."

"Who says I can't?"

"I thought your injury was too serious."

"I don't know that yet," he said as they followed the train of traffic onto Main Street.

The rain was roaring down now, plunking hard on the hood of the truck, nearly obliterating the taillights in front of them.

One by one, the vehicles turned off or sped up and pulled away as the road widened out of town.

Soon, it was dark and bleak up ahead. The hills and sky were black on black, the darkness swallowing the beam of his headlights. But he knew the road. It would narrow at the forks, winding its way along the valley wall to the ranch gates.

"But there's a possibility."

"A lot of things are possible." He wasn't ready to play worst-case scenario just yet.

"And some things are likely."

He sent her a frown. "What is it you're really asking?"

"I guess if you've thought about a path forward." She paused. "Everybody needs that in their life."

He turned the tables. "And, what's yours?"

Her life had just been upended. If she wanted to get philosophical about something, they could get philosophical about her future. He slanted a gaze at her profile, illuminated by the dashboard lights.

"Touché," she said, with a half smile.

He didn't feel as good as he should have on scoring the conversational point. "Doesn't feel so great, does it?"

"The answer is, I don't know. I don't know my future plans yet." She gave a little shrug. "Carmel, LA, maybe somewhere completely new."

"LA?" He'd pegged her for a city girl, and it looked like he'd been right.

"I have a good friend there."

"It's a big place."

"It's a huge place. I don't know if I'm ready for a city that big. I liked Carmel. But it's small. The wellness community there is even smaller."

"And the ex is still there." He let the statement hang, still wondering if part of her hoped for a reconciliation.

"That's the deal breaker."

"So, you don't want to see him?"

"He's what chased me out in the first place."

"So, that's a no?" Dallas was looking for absolute certainty here.

"It's a hard no."

A weight lifted from his chest, and he grinned.

"You're happy my—"

The truck gave a deafening bang and jolted hard left, yanking the steering wheel from his grip.

Dallas swore, wrestling for control as the truck slid sideways through the mud.

Sierra gasped, then went silent.

He pumped the brakes and steered into the skid, finally bringing the truck to a stop at an angle across the road.

"*What* was that?" she asked, a tremor in her voice.

"We've got a flat."

"A flat tire did all that?" She peered out the windshield and side window, like she thought she might find another explanation.

"In this mud, yes. And it was a blowout." He hit the hazard lights and shut off the engine. With the curve of the road and the brush on the hillside, if anyone came along they were sitting ducks.

"Wow," she said. "That was—I don't know—you did good."

"We didn't crash," he said, feeling grateful for that much as his alarm subsided and his heart rate settled back to normal. A steep valley dropped off on one side of the road with a sheer mountainside on the other.

"Should we call someone?" she asked.

He gave her a look of incomprehension. "Call who for what?"

"Like the auto club for a tire change."

Dallas gestured to himself. "Around here, I'm the guy you call. There's a jack and a spare in the back."

It was sure the wrong night to have left his Stetson at home.

"Can you do it?" she asked.

He scoffed at the question. "Change a tire?"

"With your shoulder," she elaborated.

He'd forgotten about his shoulder for a moment. "Sure." He'd wrangle his way through it. Even if they had cell service out here, there was no way he was calling for help.

"Can I help you?" she offered.

He took in her dress and shoes. "No."

She seemed to glean his meaning and glanced down at herself. "I guess I'm not dressed for it. But you're all dressed up too."

"Sacrifices must be made." He could live with ruining his pants and shirt. He'd had them for years already. And there wasn't much call for dressing up in his life lately.

"If you're sure." She raked her teeth over her bottom lip.

She looked delicate and a little defeated sitting there in the dark and the rain, yellow hazards blinking around her. He couldn't help remembering another vulnerable woman on another stormy night.

Man, he hated this road.

Lightning flashed bright, and the thunder cracked hard enough to rattle the truck. The rain came down harder, clattering off the hood and plastering the windshield.

"If we wait, maybe the storm will calm down," Sierra suggested.

"We can't sit here in the middle of the road."

The precariousness of their position seemed to dawn on her.

"The hazard lights will help," he said to reassure her. "But if someone comes around the curve at speed, it'll be a problem."

"Should we get away from the truck?"

"And stand out in the rain?"

She didn't have a ready answer for that.

"Sit tight," he said. "I'll make this quick."

"But your shoulder."

"Will survive." What had to be done, had to be done. He opened the door to a face-full of water.

He used his left hand to wrangle the jack and the spare. But he needed both hands to jack up the truck—a frustratingly messy process in the mud.

The whole thing took a toll on his shoulder, but he got it done and climbed back inside.

"You okay?" Sierra asked, looking worried.

"Fine." He might be wet, cold and sore, but Sierra was here with him, and he knew now that she wasn't hung up on her ex. He'd had way worse days than this.

Eight

Sierra was both relieved and sorry to be back at the ranch. Changing the tire had clearly taken a toll on Dallas. Wet, looking exhausted and with a telltale white patch at the tense corners of his mouth, he was quiet for the rest of the drive.

He opened the front door and stood back for her to go inside. His hair was soaked, his white shirt plastered to his chest, mud marring his forearms and the rolled-up sleeves.

"That took a while." McKinney greeted them from the great room, a twinkle of curiosity in her eyes.

She was sitting on an armchair, her feet stretched out on a brown leather ottoman. Still in her party dress, she had a glass of brandy in her hand.

"Flat tire," Dallas said. "We'll need a new spare for the black 250."

"I'll let Willis know," Austin said from a chair cornerwise to McKinney. "He's doing a run to town tomorrow."

Sierra expected Dallas to elaborate on the incident. It had been more than a simple flat tire.

Instead, he gestured for her to go into the great room.

"Brandy?" Austin asked Sierra, coming to his feet.

"Sure." Unwinding before bed seemed like a good idea.

Lightning continued to flash above the mountains and thunder clapped over the peak of the house as she sat down in one of the four armchairs. They were leather, soft and comfortable, with plenty of room to curl up.

She slipped her shoes from her tired feet and bent her knees onto the cushion.

Dallas helped himself to a brandy, then perched on the edge of a chair. It looked like he was keeping his muddy clothes away from the furniture.

Austin brought her a large snifter with a generous measure of the deep amber liquid.

She could already smell the sweet nutty scent. "Thanks."

"It's a grand rare sherry cask," McKinney said.

"Does Dad know we're drinking it?" Dallas asked as he took a hearty swig.

Austin shrugged without concern it seemed and sat back down. "It's not like we'll run out."

McKinney grinned while Sierra swirled the drink in the bulbous glass, enjoying the aroma a moment longer.

"Your funeral," Dallas said.

"You worry too much," Austin responded.

"Are we okay drinking it?" Sierra asked, reluctant to participate in something dubious. She was a guest here, and Garrett was her ultimate host.

"Nothing for you to worry about," Dallas said.

"You make him sound unreasonable," McKinney complained.

"Wouldn't want to do that," Dallas said into his glass with more than a touch of irony.

Sierra took a sip, and the flavors bloomed in her mouth. "Wow."

"Right?" McKinney asked with a grin. "This is why we pilfer the good stuff."

"At least you're admitting it now," Dallas said.

"There's at least a case still left," Austin said, smirking as he swirled his own glass.

"I feel like I'm committing a crime," Sierra joked. But she took another sip of the wonderful brandy.

"Nobody's going to jail," Austin said and polished off his drink. "But I am turning in. Morning comes early for some of us."

"Is that a dig?" Dallas asked, arching a brow as Austin rose to his feet.

"Nobody wants you to keep up except you," Austin countered. "Take it easy, man."

"I'll be up on time," Dallas said.

"I'm off too," McKinney said and stood. "But sit tight and finish your drink, Sierra. Sleep in a few hours tomorrow. I know I will. So will Austin." She gave her brother an arched look. "He's just trying to sound dedicated."

"I am dedicated," Austin said good-naturedly.

Sierra took another sip, but she was less than halfway through the brandy, and she didn't feel right about rushing such a treat. Then she saw the conspiratorial sparkle in McKinney's eyes, and realized she was giving Sierra an opportunity for a cozy chat with Dallas.

As Sierra and Austin headed up the staircase, Dallas polished off his brandy and rose.

So much for that idea.

But instead of leaving, he poured himself some more. Then he turned and held up the rounded, gold-adorned bottle to her.

"No thanks." She lifted her glass to show him she had plenty left.

He settled into a chair.

She hoped he'd open the conversation himself, so she could take her clue from that. But he sat in silence, gazing at a hurricane lamp set in the middle of the square coffee table in the center of the chair grouping.

"You feeling okay?" she asked.

He looked her way, blinking like she'd pulled him out of a trance.

"Your shoulder," she clarified. "It can't have been easy changing the tire."

He flexed his shoulder and flinched. "It's fine."

"That was about the worst lie I've ever heard."

He dipped his chin and gazed skeptically. "Really? The worst?"

"You don't have to be brave."

"You make me sound like a seven-year-old with a boo-boo."

She hated that she was getting this so wrong. "I didn't mean it that way. I know you're in pain. You're in a lot of pain." She set down her brandy and came to her feet. "Let me."

"You don't have to."

"Yes, I do." Relieving someone's pain—whether it was physical or emotional—was a calling for her. It always had been. It was the reason she'd gone into the wellness profession.

She stood poised above his shoulder.

"You really don't need to do that."

"Stop fighting me." She put her hands on his shoulder.

"Fine." He sounded resigned.

"This won't hurt a—" She stopped herself. "Okay, it'll hurt. But it'll help too."

"I know."

"Good." She gently explored the tension in his muscle fibers.

It didn't take long for her to feel frustrated. She needed a proper table, a good massage oil and access to his bare skin.

He didn't complain when she unbuttoned the top of his shirt and loosened it around his neck. And he leaned forward in the chair, but he was still bracing himself with his arms.

"You need to lie down somewhere," she told him, looking to the short sofa before dismissing it. "And I need some massage oil, anything will do. Some olive oil in the kitchen, maybe?" She was up for getting creative.

"I have no idea."

"Coconut oil would work. Something with lavender would be better. I like jojoba."

"Oh, sure. Like I want to smell like lavender."

"Maybe sandalwood or balsam for you."

"I think there's a bottle of something down in the gym." Sierra paused. "You have a gym?"

"There's a sauna and a steam room downstairs too."

"You have a downstairs?" She had a hard time imagining there was even more to this monstrously large house than what she'd already seen.

"What did you think was behind the wall at the hot tub?"

"I don't know." She hadn't wondered about it at all. "Can we go get it? The oil, I mean."

"We can." He rolled to his feet. "The stairs are just down the hall from the wine cellar."

She followed him to a door at the end of the hallway that opened to an L-shaped staircase.

At the bottom of the stairs, Dallas turned on some pe-

rimeter lighting, softly illuminating the hushed, cavernous room.

She could see a treadmill, a stationary bike and an el-
liptical machine. An elaborate weight training area took up
one end, and there was a pair of raw cedar doors to what
she assumed were the sauna and steam rooms.

But what caught her eye were the thick workout mats
stacked beside a mirrored wall.

"In here, I think," Dallas said, heading for a short hallway.

Two big bathrooms were off opposite sides of the hall.
In one of them he located a bottle of blended oil.

"I have no idea how long this has been here."

"It won't go bad." She took it from his hands and gestured to the gym. "You can lie down on one of those mats."

Her request clearly gave him pause, but it was hard to
tell why.

"Have I steered you wrong yet?" she asked.

"No."

"Then, trust me."

"Okay." He drew in a breath. "Fine." Then he started
for the mats. "Let's do this."

Sierra liked the progress she was feeling in Dallas's
shoulder muscles. She'd gotten a couple of knots to release
right here during the session, and the tangled fibers near
his shoulder blade were finally smoothing out.

His skin had gone pink in the soft lighting, and she
could almost feel the healing blood flow increasing as
she worked.

"Can I increase the pressure?" she asked, keeping her
voice soft so as not to disturb his tranquil state.

"Sure," he mumbled, his eyes closed.

She smiled at that, going slowly, making sure he didn't

tense up, focusing on the healthier muscles around the injury site.

After a while, she stilled her hands. "Can you turn over?"

He rolled slowly onto his back and opened his eyes.

"You've been kneeling on the floor for a long time," he said with concern.

"I'm fine." There was room on the spongy mat for her knees. "Just relax. You're doing great."

He cracked a small smile. "I'm not *doing* anything."

Warmed by his expression, she couldn't help smiling back. "You're healing."

"This is the first time I've come close to liking it."

"Then I'm succeeding."

"You're succeeding. Anybody ever tell you, you have magic hands?"

Some clients had said things along those lines. But she shook her head no, not wanting to give hints about her real profession.

"You have magic hands." He traced a line from her forearm, over her palm to the tip of her middle finger. "Magic."

"Your parasympathetic nervous system has engaged."

"I don't know what that means."

"It means more serotonin and dopamine for you."

"Yeah?" He wrapped his hand around hers. "I seem to like those things."

"You're supposed to like them."

He slid his hand to her elbow, urging her closer.

"Dallas," she warned, even as she craved another of his kisses.

"Yes?" he whispered, as he drew her to him.

"I'm not finished." But she didn't resist his steady pressure.

"I don't care."

"You'll—"

His lips brushed hers.

Like it had on the patio, the kiss started slow, tantaliz-ingly light, but provoking a powerful reaction deep within her.

She kissed him back, folding into his arms, bringing her breasts to his chest and opening to the kisses that deep-ened between them.

Desire rushed to her chest. Arousal pulsed its way through her limbs.

In no time, she was lying flush against him, moving her kisses from his lips to his temple, to the top of his head as his kisses made their way down her neck to her shoulders, leaving damp spots behind.

He drew down her zipper.

She arched against him, feeling the bulges and hollows of his body settling to hers like the final pieces of a diffi-cult puzzle. There was nothing to stop them this time. She didn't want anything to stop them this time.

She drew her arms from the straps of her dress, letting the fabric shimmer to her waist.

He gazed at her breasts. Then his eyes fluttered closed, and his hand cupped one mound.

She gasped with an indrawn breath, shards of pleasure jolting to her core and out along her limbs.

"You are gorgeous," he said. Then he was kissing her again, hugging her close, bare skin to bare skin.

His fingertips trailed up her thighs, and she held her breath as they circled closer and closer.

She pressed her palms on his chest, smoothing them over the curve of his pecs and his washboard abs. She brushed the button of his pants. Flicking it open was a point of no return.

She took a steadying breath, her chest filling with anticipation as she pushed the button through the hole and lifted the tab of his zipper.

He reached her panties with a light touch, and a swift bolt of passion raised goose bumps on her skin.

"Oh," she gasped.

He groaned. The arm around her waist tightened, and he slipped his finger past the lace band at the top of her leg.

Urgent arousal took over, blurring her thoughts and her vision while a buzz came up in her ears.

They gave in to the inevitable, shucking his pants and pulling off her panties.

More than ready, she moved one leg over his body.

"Hey." He wrapped his hand around her arm and tried to move from beneath her.

"No," she said, firmly, putting her palm on his chest. It was a gesture, since she couldn't possibly hold him down. "You're injured."

"I'm not that injured," he said.

But he stayed put as she settled on top of him. "I say again, have I ever steered you wrong?"

"No, ma'am," he said, relaxing, lying back and focusing on her body above him.

"Then trust me now."

"Yes, ma'am."

His hands bracketed her hips, supporting her movements.

Pure, unadulterated ecstasy pushed its way through her, igniting every synapse, every nerve, filling her with steadily building pleasure.

His hands covered her breasts.

Her body heated, arousal rising higher as they moved together.

His lips parted, and his eyes darkened, smoldering and

smoky. He was such a beautiful man, an exquisite example of a sexy male.

Their gazes met and locked.

His breathing grew labored, and her lungs struggled to keep up.

She held his compelling gaze as long as she could, but then she threw back her head as a kaleidoscope of bright colors danced in front of her. The buzz in her ears turned to a roaring crescendo.

Then the world imploded around her, waves of pleasure convulsing over and over again.

It took her a minute to realize she held Dallas's shoulders in a death grip.

She snatched her hands back. "Sorry."

He gave a breathless chuckle. "Didn't feel a thing."

She tilted her head back down to give him a playful admonishing look. "Nothing?" She took a breath. "Not a thing?"

"Nothing that hurt," he carefully stated.

Bathed in a rosy afterglow, she gave him a smile. She knew regret was an inevitable part of this equation. But not yet. Not yet.

She leaned forward, and he folded her into his arms, lying there until her heart rate approached something resembling normal.

"That wasn't supposed to happen," she said, when it seemed like he wasn't going to say anything.

He gently smoothed her hair, seeming to think for a moment before speaking. "It seemed natural to me."

She considered his answer. "I suppose the not knowing is over with now." At least there was that. The idea of trying to help him around all that simmering sexual tension had been daunting. But the dam was broken. Maybe that was a good thing.

"That's one way to look at it," he said.

She wanted to ask him the other way. She wanted to take this moment to probe more deeply into his psyche. But she knew that would be wrong.

Her personal relationship with Dallas had to remain strictly separate from her professional one. Even though he didn't know they had a professional relationship. And even though this had to be the absolute end of their personal relationship.

With regret, she laid her palm on his cheek, then kissed him tenderly on the lips. "It's really late."

"Who cares?"

"We will." She sat up. "When we try to work tomorrow."

He put his hands on her shoulders. "McKinney told you to sleep in."

She moved off him and adjusted her dress. "Everyone else will be up. You said it yourself. It's hard enough for me to fit in without being treated like a princess."

He sat up. "Things were different when I said that."

"Why?" She couldn't help an amused smile as she sought out her panties. "Because this time you want me to have special treatment?"

He frowned.

"You were right, Dallas." She touched his hand. "I can't be a princess."

"I'm sorry I ever said that."

"Don't be sorry."

"I misjudged you."

"Not really."

"Sierra."

Back together now, she stood up. "Good night, Dallas."

"But?" He spread his hands in a gesture of perplexity. "We can't just ignore this."

"We did before."

"That was a kiss. This was—"

"More than a kiss. I know. I was there." But she didn't see that she had any choice. She'd made a promise to McKinney, and she intended to keep it. That promise was her whole reason for being here.

Dallas liked working with young horses. He liked everything about it—from the give-and-take of groundwork and handling to settling the animals into a saddle. It took concentration and patience. Every horse was different, each its own challenge and reward.

In the northwest round pen, cowhand Caden Renick was rubbing a flexible bareback pad on Treasure, a two-year-old buckskin gelding.

"He's come a long way," Austin said from where he stood next to Dallas at the fence.

"From what?" Dallas asked with some surprise, watching while the colt shied to the side.

"Whoa," Caden said in a low voice, slacking off on the lead rope to give Treasure a chance to settle down.

"I meant Caden," Austin said, a smile in his voice.

"Oh. True." Dallas would agree with that.

Caden had talked his way onto the Hawkes ranch ten years ago as an absolute greenhorn. They'd only kept him on in those early days because he made up in hard work what he lacked in skill. He was the first up in the morning and the last to quit on the day.

Their father had admired his pluck.

"Still works his butt off," Austin added.

"He has a good touch," Dallas said.

The two men watched while Caden made long, smooth strokes with the bareback pad from Treasure's withers to his haunches.

"Late night last night?" Austin asked, the studied nonchalance in his voice tweaking Dallas's radar.

"It was for all of us," Dallas answered, still watching Caden and the horse.

"Saw the great room was empty." Austin paused. "At two a.m."

Dallas sent his brother a penetrating look. "You making some kind of a point?"

"You didn't come upstairs until after three."

"And?"

Austin shifted to face him. "And Sierra."

"What about Sierra?"

"Don't deny you were with her."

"What if I was?"

"She's an employee." Disapproval was clear in Austin's tone.

"She was massaging my shoulder." Dallas had no intention of sharing anything more. It was nobody's business, and also irrelevant since Sierra had insisted it be a one-time thing.

Austin arched a skeptical brow.

Dallas flexed his shoulder, showing off the range of motion. "She knows what she's doing. The massage made a huge difference for me."

Austin studied Dallas's expression intently, as if he was trying to deduce more information. After a moment, he seemed to back off. "I'm glad to hear that."

"And she's getting better at ranch work," Dallas added. "Like Caden. She tries hard. She's learning."

"Call me irrational, but I don't see a future cowhand in that woman."

"You never know."

"Don't get your hopes up, brother. One way or another, she's not long for this ranch."

Dallas had meant Sierra could learn, not that she might stay. "My hopes have nothing to do with this. And I'm not staying either."

"Yeah? Well, your thirtieth birthday's coming up."

Dallas clenched his jaw. It was a grim reality that the date came around every year. On the road, he could ignore it. Here, it was going to be much harder.

"I'm getting stronger by the day," he said.

"Good."

"I might return to the circuit early. You know, get my feet under me and find my old rhythm before I start to compete.

Austin rocked back. "You can't be thinking about rodeoing again."

"I can, and I am."

"You intend to hurt yourself even worse?"

"I intend to win money and buckles."

Treasure whinnied and kicked up a cloud of dust as Caden put pressure on the cinch. The colt pranced sideways, keeping the cowboy's hands full in the pen.

"Does Dad know about this?" Austin asked.

"I can't imagine he doesn't." Dallas hadn't made any secret of his plans.

"The doc said you should retire from the ring."

"They always say that." If every rodeo cowboy took every doctor's most cautious advice, there'd be no sport left at all.

"You need to start thinking long term, brother."

"I am thinking long term."

Austin coughed a cold laugh. "All the way to November?"

"The rest of this year's circuit is the first part of long term."

Treasure bucked repeatedly against the tightened bareback pad, causing an even bigger ruckus.

Austin called out to Caden. "That's probably enough for today."

Caden gave an easy nod of agreement. He stroked Treasure's neck and withers, talking low to the animal as he removed the pad before gently leading the colt to the gate.

Another cowboy entered the pen with an appaloosa filly.

"I'm not trying to pressure you," Austin said to Dallas.

It was Dallas's turn to cough out a laugh. "I can tell," he said sarcastically.

"I just want to get you thinking."

"Thinking is about all I do these days."

Dallas needed to get back full-time in the saddle. When a man was working hard and sweating over a challenge, especially when the stakes were high, he didn't have time for thoughts or regrets.

"It's a big ranch," Austin said. "Times are changing, and it's going to take a big family to run it."

Dallas could hear echoes of his father's arguments, and he still wasn't buying it. "From what I've seen, you'll be able to run the whole operation from a computer terminal."

"It's not that simple. And your attitude sucks."

"Maybe so. But it's your dream, not mine."

"It's an obligation."

The criticism stung Dallas more than he cared to admit. But he quashed the feeling. Guilt was the Hawkes family's weapon of choice. "Only if you let it be one."

Austin could make all the choices he wanted.

Dallas would stick with his own.

Sierra had taken to visiting Cedric whenever she had a spare minute. And Cedric had taken to visiting her back.

She slipped through the gate into the home paddock, watching as the elegant horse trotted enthusiastically toward her through the waving meadow grass. The backdrop of evergreen mountains and crystal blue sky gave the impression of paradise.

Three weeks ago, his looming size would have terrified her. She wouldn't have entered the paddock at all. And, if she had, she'd be scrambling through the gate as soon as she saw him coming, backing well away from the fence for safety.

But now she was happy to see Cedric's enthusiasm. It made her feel good to know she had a friend in the elderly animal.

"There's a boy," she crooned as he slowed and settled to a stop beside her.

He presented his neck for a pat and whinnied softly when she complied. He eased ahead to give her access to his shoulder, broadly hinting at what he wanted. It was easy enough to guess, and she started a little massage.

Cedric nodded his head in what she interpreted to be approval.

"You like that a whole lot," she said, using both hands on his heated and slightly dusty coat.

The horse blew softly through its nostrils.

"You've sure got a fan there," McKinney said from behind Sierra.

Sierra grinned over her shoulder at McKinney's approach on horseback on the opposite side of the fence. "This boy deserves it."

"My retirement should be so good." McKinney dismounted, wrapping the horse's reins around a rail.

"He's such a pussycat," Sierra said as Cedric stretched under her hands.

"I didn't know you massaged animals too."

"I don't. I mean I didn't. This just sort of evolved." From the day she'd given Cedric a bath, Sierra had fallen into the habit of impromptu massages.

It was easy to guess that aging horses developed aches and pains just like aging people. Her geriatric patients had some of the best outcomes from regular massage treatments and nutritional advice.

Sierra believed strongly in the power of human touch.

McKinney cracked the gate and slipped into the paddock.

"What's up with you today?" Sierra asked, taking in McKinney's hat, chaps, bandanna and the rope slung over her saddle horn.

"We're moving one of the herds down to vaccinate the calves. I'm on deck to help with the last mile."

"So, real cowgirl work."

"That's right. Herding and roping."

"You like it, don't you?" Sierra couldn't help comparing McKinney's attitude with Dallas's.

Her friend seemed completely fulfilled and at home on the ranch. So much so that Sierra was envious. It must be nice to have such a solid sense of belonging.

Not that Sierra could ever picture herself roping and riding. Forget the skills, she didn't have the strength. She and McKinney were close to the same size, but McKinney was in much better shape.

The woman had always seemed to have stamina to burn. She was a marvel at beach volleyball. Sierra had never seen a leap or a spike like McKinney's.

"I heard you used your skills on Dallas," McKinney said, her tone curious, expression searching.

Sierra stilled, hit with twin shots of guilt and anxiety, wondering how much McKinney had heard and where she'd heard it. She scrambled to formulate an answer.

"I say, way to go." McKinney sounded surprisingly enthusiastic. "Did you get him talking?"

Sierra focused on Cedric again to hide her embarrassment. "Where did you hear?"

"He told Austin."

"Austin." Sierra was surprised Dallas would share with his brother, especially after they'd both agreed it wouldn't happen again.

"You and your magic massage," McKinney carried on.

Sierra glanced her way, trying to decide if the massage was all McKinney knew about, or if she was working her way up to something more.

"Works on all manner of animals apparently," McKinney said breezily.

A breath of relief burst from Sierra. It was only the massage.

"So, what did you two talk about?" McKinney asked. "Are you making progress?"

"He didn't say very much." That was true. "The massage was for his injury."

McKinney looked disappointed.

"It works for emotional bonding too," Sierra offered, swallowing her guilt.

McKinney nodded thoughtfully. "Of course. Great approach. Slow and steady. I like it."

"It's all connected." Sierra launched into a speech she gave her clients. "Ease the physical pain, and you ease the emotional pain along with it."

"Heads up," McKinney said. "Eight o'clock."

Sierra was confused. "Eight o'clock?"

"He's coming up behind us."

Sierra looked over her shoulder once more to see Dallas striding across the dirt runout. His Stetson was pulled low, his plaid shirt stretched across his broad chest, and his faded blue jeans and battered boots made him every inch the sexy cowboy.

Her skin heated at the sight of him, reminded of their lovemaking two nights ago and the erotic dreams that had haunted her ever since.

"Morning," he said, his voice making her reaction more acute.

"You riding out with us?" McKinney asked him.

"Thinking about it." He answered McKinney, but his gaze was on Sierra.

His eyes were bedroom soft, his expression heated. If he wasn't careful, he was going to give them away.

"Feeling better?" McKinney asked her brother. "I heard Sierra gave you a massage."

Dallas broke eye contact with Sierra and shifted to his sister. "Is that what passes for family gossip now?"

"Isn't she great?"

"She is great." The sexy edge to Dallas's voice rang clearly in Sierra's ears.

"She's mostly inept," Sierra put in briskly, turning her attention back to Cedric. She was afraid her own expression might give something away to McKinney.

They both laughed behind her, even though it wasn't a joke.

"Get her to give you another massage," McKinney said to Dallas. "I mean, if the first one worked for you, why not?"

"That's up to Sierra," Dallas said.

"Oh, she won't mind," McKinney said blithely.

"Don't put her in such an awkward position."

Sierra silently thanked Dallas for that. The last thing the two of them needed was more alone time and her hands on his bare skin.

A memory bloomed, and her skin prickled with heat once again.

"Take the help," McKinney told her brother with conviction. "Don't throw up unnecessary barriers."

Sierra understood what McKinney was trying to do—give Sierra more time to talk with Dallas and figure out what made him tick. It was a smart strategy. It wasn't McKinney's fault Sierra had let things get out of hand.

"Sure." Sierra turned, putting a bright note in her voice. "I'd be happy to give you another massage."

Dallas's brow rose in surprise. "You would?"

"Yes."

"Are you sure?"

She wished there was an expression that conveyed she only meant it for medicinal purposes. But she couldn't figure out how to arrange her features to silently tell him that.

"Great!" McKinney said with enthusiasm. Then she headed back through the gate. "I'll leave you two to work out the details."

She retrieved her horse's reins, stepped into the stirrup and remounted. "We're riding out in half an hour," she told Dallas as she settled her Stetson and kicked the horse into a trot.

Dallas and Sierra gazed at each other in uncomfortable silence.

He was the first to break it. "We can tell her you changed your mind."

Sierra shook her head. "I'll do it."

If she didn't, McKinney would ask why. And Sierra knew she could help his physical healing. She wasn't going to hold that back. Plus, she also wanted to learn more about his emotional state. She simply wanted to do all that without ending up in his arms or his bed.

"Really." He looked pleased, and a glint came into his eyes, sending her heart into an unwelcome flutter.

"Dallas." She was warning him, but she was warning herself too.

"What?"

"You know we agreed." She put her burgeoning energy into the horse massage.

"I know one of us agreed."

She gave him a pointed look.

He held his palms up in surrender. "I absolutely respect your decision."

Cedric took a side step, then another, turning to show his other side to Sierra.

"He's got you pegged," Dallas said.

"He knows exactly what he wants." Sierra started on the opposite shoulder.

Dallas didn't answer, but she realized she'd left herself wide open to him telling her exactly what he wanted too.

Instead, he stayed silent while the breeze whistled its way through a nearby aspen grove and a few shouting voices carried from the round pen on the other side of the barn.

A robin fluttered down to perch on a fence post, twittering as he surveyed the ground.

"Your massage did me a world of good," he said.

She'd known it would. And she knew she could do even more for him. But she couldn't fall into his arms again, no matter how badly she wanted to.

Nine

"It can't be in the gym again," Sierra told Dallas with a shake of her head.

The night's dinner was over, and he'd caught up with her outside on the main patio.

He understood her stance and had no intention of pushing her. Their attraction had clearly been mutual that night—still was, if the shimmer in her eyes was anything to go by. But he completely respected her decision.

"The games room has plenty of space," he said.

They were alone enough to have a private conversation but visible from the house with a couple of gardeners in sight near the pond.

"Where's the games room?"

"It's next to the gym. Plenty roomy."

"So, alone again in the quiet depths of the basement?" She made a good point.

"What about the view room?" He suggested an alternative. "It's off the wine tasting room and partially open to that hallway."

"Dallas?" His dad's rumbling voice sounded from the open doors to the dining room. "Got a minute?"

Sierra's eyes widened and she drew back.

"Don't," Dallas told her. "We're not doing anything wrong here."

Her lips compressed.

"We're not," he repeated. Just because they wanted to keep their personal relationship private didn't make it wrong. And everyone was going to know about the massages soon enough.

"Can I speak with you?" his dad added, sounding impatient.

"Go," Sierra said, easing back even farther.

"Fine." Dallas answered his father, frustrated by the interruption. He spoke more softly to Sierra. "Later?"

She nodded.

"Good."

As she headed for the cobblestone path, Dallas made his way toward his father's unsmiling face.

"Something wrong?" If something was off the rails, Dallas would rather know about it up front.

"No. Join me in the den."

The den didn't seem like the room to choose if nothing was wrong. It was a serious room—hushed and private, with a low hewn-wood ceiling and five black leather chairs around a smoked glass table.

Dallas followed his father into the den to find Austin already there at the table.

He gave his brother a *what's up* look, but Austin's expression was neutral.

"Close the door," his father said.

"What is this?" Dallas asked, glancing warily from one to the other.

"Can you just—" His father seemed to catch himself, erasing the impatience from his voice. "Can we all sit down first?"

Dallas closed the door and took a seat facing his father.

"Your thirtieth birthday," his father opened.

Dallas felt the words like a gut punch. He started to rise, wanting nothing to do with whatever conversation they were about to have here.

Austin gave him a hard stare. "It's not that."

"What else would it be?" Dallas's birthday was a dark day for all of them, since it marked their mother's death.

The impatience came back in their father's tone. "She's gone, Dallas. It's time to move on—for all of us."

The rest of the family might have moved on, but Dallas would never move on from the guilt.

"Dad," Austin said in a warning tone.

His father took a beat before speaking to Dallas. "I wanted to talk to you because, on your thirtieth birthday, in accordance with your grandfather's will—"

Dallas drew back with surprise, looking to Austin again for some insight.

"—you inherit title to a share of the Hawkes ranch property."

It was Dallas's turn to take a beat. "What are you talking about?" His first and only thought was it was a trick to keep him here.

His father continued. "It was your grandfather's hope, his wish, his dream, that his grandchildren would keep the ranch intact and run it together, protecting it for future generations. But he knew he couldn't force you to do it. He knew it had to be your choice. So, he took a chance."

"My choice is to leave," Dallas pointed out.

"Yet you're here now," Austin responded.

"Temporarily."

"Fifteen thousand acres," his father said flatly.

Dallas blinked, thinking he must not have heard right.

"I took the southeast section," Austin said. "From Bromegrass Ridge to the river bend at the highway."

Dallas gaped at his brother, trying to make sense of the conversation. "You—"

"As the oldest, I had first choice," Austin said with a trace of humor. "So, why not?"

"Legally, it's to do with as you please," their father said.

Dallas looked at his dad again, brow furrowing in confusion. This had been hanging out there all these years?

"Pick your land—"

"And stay," Dallas finished for his father, a trace of bitterness in his voice. He came to his feet and took a few paces. "Stay here forever is what you're saying."

His father's voice turned sharp. "Stay, go, wallow in self-pity. I can't force you to do anything."

Dallas squared his shoulders and straightened his spine, stung by the unwarranted criticism. He turned to glare at his father.

"You can even sell it if you want," his father finished.

The idea hit Dallas like a lightning bolt. He could sell his land, pocket a small fortune and—

"He's not going to sell," Austin said, sounding disgusted by the suggestion.

"Look at his face," their father said.

"You can't break up the land," Austin warned.

Dallas never would have considered it. He couldn't imagine the Hawkes ranch being anything other than what it had been all these years. But it was a tantalizing idea, cutting ties and never coming back to the sights and sounds that ate away at his soul.

"I have to think about this," he said. His mind was reeling from the implications.

Austin shot to his feet. "You *can't* be serious."

"You," Dallas said, frustrated that his brother hadn't given him a heads-up. "You've owned that much of the ranch for over a year now? You knew this was coming for me?"

"It wasn't my place to say anything."

His father warned Dallas in a gruff voice. "And it's not your place to say anything to Tyler or McKinney. Their time will come. Your decision is yours and yours alone."

"Do you want him to leave?" Austin asked their father.

"He knows his own mind," their father said, looking levelly into Dallas's eyes.

The room went dead still and silent. And for the first time in his life, Dallas felt like his father understood him, as if his father would truly respect Dallas's choice to stay or leave. It was the oddest sensation.

"It's our heritage," Austin said with finality. "Ours and our children's, and their children's children."

"Back off," Dallas ground out. He didn't need Austin or anyone else emphasizing family duty while he thought this through.

But Austin wasn't finished. "Keep *that* in mind while you're *thinking* about this."

Sierra was surprised by the level of tension in Dallas's body. He was stiff as a board all over.

They'd rolled out a sleeping pad on a heavy rectangular table in the view room. She could see where the place got its name. West facing, the fields and mountains were beautiful. And the sunset was spectacular.

"What's going on with you today?" She hated being

so blunt, but his emotional state was blocking her ability to help him.

He didn't answer.

"Is it me?" She wondered if they needed to clear the air, try to diffuse the sexual tension.

"No," he said.

"You sure?"

"I'm sure."

"Something else, then?"

"No."

"Dallas, you're completely tensed up." She massaged a little harder, trying to break through.

"Ouch," he complained.

"I can barely work here." She knew she couldn't force him to talk. And forcing him to do anything would be counterproductive. "What about some music?" She had some soothing instrumentals on her phone.

"I don't want music."

She moved to his lower back, thinking she'd start somewhere that wouldn't cause him any pain and work her way up.

"What are you doing way down there?" he asked.

"Trying to get you to relax."

"I am relaxed."

"That was the second-worst lie I've ever heard," she lightly joked.

He didn't respond.

She massaged his lumbar area a while longer, not making any real progress.

"Do you want to talk about it?" she asked softly.

"No."

"*Will* you talk about it? I mean, you don't have to like the talking to have it help."

"It's not going to help."

"So, you admit there's something going on?"

He heaved a huge sigh.

"I'll take that as a yes," she said.

"Anybody ever tell you you're stubborn?"

"Right back at you, cowboy."

"I'm steadfast. And that's only because I know what I want." He paused. "Don't want. What I don't want."

She gave the conversation a rest, working her way up his spine to the inside of his shoulder blade, sticking to areas that were pain free.

"And, what's that?" she dared asked.

"It's not a secret."

"You don't want to be here." She made the most obvious guess.

"First prize to you."

"Have you ever stopped to think about why?"

"I don't have to think about it."

She let a few beats go by. "Because?"

He waited a long time before answering. "Because I know what I did."

Her heart lifted at his answer. It sounded dark and sad. But it was more specific than he'd ever been before.

She was impatient to ask more but didn't want him to shut down again. So, she carried on with the massage, slowly and gradually, until at last she felt him relax.

She opened her mouth to prompt him, but he muttered into the sleeping pad before she could speak.

"I was always a good cowboy," he said.

As she waited for more, she couldn't help picturing Dallas as a child and then a teenager. He was smart and energetic and had likely always been that way. She didn't doubt he excelled at riding and roping and everything else that came along with living on a ranch.

"So were Austin and Tyler. McKinney was pretty young back then."

"Back when?"

"We were teenagers. She was maybe seven or eight."

"I see." She didn't exactly see where this was going, but she wanted to keep him talking.

"Austin thought he should be in charge."

The statement didn't surprise her since Austin was the oldest brother.

"He wouldn't listen to reason. Ever. At least, that's what I thought. So, I fought his ideas. And I fought hard."

Sierra circled her thumbs closer to Dallas's injury, finding a knot and easing the pressure against it.

"We were up on Creston Ridge, me, Austin and Tyler. A storm was rolling in fast. We could see the herd of mares we'd been tracking clustered in the valley bottom. I wanted to go straight down the draw and come at them from the east. Austin wanted to go around, take the long way to skip the steep slope. But we'd have lost sight of them, and they'd have had room to run away. We'd been out for three days looking, and, you know, the storm."

Sierra realized she'd stopped massaging and prompted herself to start again.

"Tyler sided with me. It was the first time he'd ever done that. I think he was sick of sleeping on the ground and eating dried food. He didn't want to spend the night in the rain, and we didn't dare go back without the mares. Dad would have—"

She massaged the tension in his neck, waiting for him to start talking again.

"What happened?" she finally asked.

"The storm broke when we were halfway down the slope. Tyler's horse slipped in the mud. They both went down hard."

Sierra hated to ask. But she had to ask. "Were they okay?"

"Tyler was knocked unconscious, and the horse injured its leg. For a minute there—" Dallas took a shuddering breath. "For a minute there, I thought we were going to have to shoot the horse."

Sierra's stomach clenched, thinking about her bond with Cedric and how all the Hawkes ranch cowboys seemed to feel about their horses. "But you didn't?"

"No. But instead of arriving home with a valuable herd of mares, we slogged our way through a driving storm with a lame horse and an injured brother."

Someone walked past in the hallway.

Sierra didn't look to see who it was, but Dallas stopped talking.

Whoever it was continued on their way, footsteps fading.

She wanted to ask him how Tyler had fared and how his father had reacted, but she sensed he'd had enough for one day. This was a breakthrough, no matter how she looked at it.

"I was confident in the rodeo," Dallas surprised her by saying. "*Am* confident in the rodeo—intensity, unpredictability and split-second decisions. Not everybody can do that."

"Very few people can." That seemed obvious.

"It's the other," he said.

"Other?"

It was a long moment before he spoke. "My mom died on my birthday. Did McKinney ever tell you that?"

Sierra stilled her hands, her heart going out to him. "Oh, Dallas. I'm so sorry."

He didn't answer right away.

"And it's a reminder," she guessed. "Every year, your birthday is a reminder of how much you miss her."

Sierra felt him draw a very deep breath, and she searched for something comforting to say.

"Time helps," she offered.

There was a bitterness to his tone. "So they tell me."

"It's true. If you don't mind me asking, did you leave the ranch right after she died?"

"I left after high school."

"Same year?" Sierra was getting a picture here.

"Yes."

"And you don't come back much."

"Only when I have to."

"Do you think—" She hesitated, not wanting to push too hard. "Do you think you might be short-circuiting your healing process by spending so much time away?"

"No." His response was terse.

"Have you considered the value in replacing the bad memories with—"

"Are you done with the massage?" He started to sit, obviously determined to avoid the conversation.

"I'm not done." She gently pressed him back down, falling silent, working into the toughest of the knots.

He grunted.

"Is that too much pressure?"

"No. Not too much. It's good." He relaxed under her hands again.

She wasn't surprised by his response. He was tough as nails where it came to his physical recovery—less so where it came to his emotions.

The next day, Sierra's words echoed through Dallas's mind. She couldn't have been more wrong. He needed less time on the ranch, not more.

Still, he couldn't stop thinking about it.

His birthday was never cause for celebration. Out on

the circuit, he'd simply ignored it and carried on rodeoing. But today was different. It couldn't be ignored. Because of his grandfather's decades-old aspirations, Dallas had a life-altering decision to make.

He'd put it off until late in the afternoon.

But now, standing at the table in the den, his father and Austin looking on, Dallas pointed to the topographical map of the ranch, its roughly triangular shape with two arms stretching out west and the northwest.

"I'll take the White Foam Falls section, from the narrows north."

"That's not fifteen thousand acres," his father said with a frown.

"Close enough," Dallas said. It had never been his goal to own any of the property outright.

"Can't you see what he's doing?" Austin asked.

"Taking the high country. That's not the choicest land, son," his father said.

"It's my choice." Dallas stabbed his finger against the paper. "That's what I want."

"It's far and away the easiest chunk to hive off," Austin said. "He's going to sell."

Their father's gaze narrowed. "Is that your plan?"

"I don't have a plan." Dallas had known about the will's provision for less than two weeks.

"Then you're keeping your options open," Austin said.

Dallas nodded to that. He'd be a fool not to keep his options open.

"Come on, man." Austin dropped into one of the chairs with an expression of defeat. "Don't do something you can't undo."

"I don't know what I'm going to do yet." Dallas couldn't imagine tying himself permanently to the Jagged Creek Valley, coping with the gnawing pain of what might have been if he'd made a different choice that day and his mother had lived.

"What will it take?" his father asked. "To keep you in the fold?"

Dallas shook his head. "There's nothing here for me."

A muscle ticked in his father's cheek. "Your *family* is here."

"Only part of it."

"You think it's any different for the rest of us?" Austin rasped. "You don't think we miss her too?"

Dallas glared at his brother. Missing their mother was one thing. Confronting the guilt was something completely different.

"Selling is the *last* thing Grampa wanted," Austin growled.

"Then why did he do this?" Dallas hadn't asked for it. But it was a way out for him, a way permanently out.

"Worst-case scenario was splitting it up," Austin said.

"Your brother's right," their father said to Dallas.

"Isn't he always?" Dallas hadn't meant to sound petulant.

Austin lifted his hands in abject frustration.

Their father's brow furrowed. "What's that supposed to mean?"

Now that he was in the thick of it, Dallas kept going. "If only we did what Austin said all the time, everything would be just fine."

"Explain?" his father demanded.

Dallas shook his head. There was nothing to explain. It had always been that way, and everyone knew it.

"White Foam Falls," he said, pointing at the map. "That's my choice." Then he turned for the door.

"Dallas!" his father called out sharply.

But Dallas didn't stop. He stomped his way down the hall,

heading for the front door. A stop at the barn, then he'd be out in the fresh air on the open range, riding away from the argument with his family.

He was completely off the painkillers now, and after several massages and some gradual strengthening exercise, he was perfectly capable of saddling Jayden.

He silently pulled his gear from the tack room.

One look at his expression had Rudy and Ethan staying silent.

He led Jayden to a runout to saddle him up.

Sierra arrived when he was halfway through.

"Hey," she said, gently, clearly realizing something was wrong.

He didn't know if she'd come across him by accident or if someone had told her he was angry.

"Hey, yourself." He didn't stop working, tightening the girth strap.

"Happy—"

"Don't," he warned her with a dark look, then felt like a heel for snapping at her.

She swallowed. "Going someplace?"

He knew he should apologize, but he didn't want to hang around for a conversation. And Sierra was the master of dragging him into conversations.

"Yes," he told her shortly, unhooking the stirrup from the saddle horn.

"Where?"

"Out."

"Dallas."

He paused, lifting his brow and waiting.

"You're upset," she said.

"I know."

"Do you want to—"

"No." He turned and mounted up. "I want to ride."

She didn't need to cope with him when he was like this.
"We could talk for a minute."

"This isn't your problem."

"I know, but—"

"It's fine, Sierra."

"I don't mind."

"You don't?" he asked sarcastically. "Well, I do."

She gazed a moment longer, her pretty eyes narrowing with concern.

He looked away. He was far too susceptible to her brand of sympathy and persuasion. The last thing he needed right now was compassion.

She finally backed away, and he turned Jayden for the gate.

Out to the meadow and up the rise, he had to fight to keep himself from looking back.

He knew what he'd find there: Sierra in worn jeans and a purple checkerboard shirt, her honey blond hair pulled back in a braid, wisps fluttering free around her sky-blue eyes. She was a singular good thing, a blissful memory in his haze of regret. He couldn't afford to let that in right now.

Then he was over the rise, across the meadow, headed northeast just as far as Jayden wanted to run. The main house was in the center of the Hawkes ranch. A man could ride for days in any direction and never leave the family land.

Hours later, they trotted into the setting sun and came up on the wide dirt trail that led to Spruce Grouse Lake.

It was cooler in the long streams of dappled shade, and he slowed Jayden to a walk.

Dallas lifted his hat and wiped his brow with his sleeve.

He'd been fighting off thoughts of his mother all day. But they crowded in now—the storm, the accident and every decision he'd made after getting out of bed that fateful morning. A twist here, a turn there. So many things could have changed the outcome.

Jayden twitched beneath him, telling him he was tensing up. The horse was right. Dallas was on his way down the rabbit hole again.

He brought up an image of Sierra instead, her smile, her warm eyes, their glint of determination when she found something difficult, and her self-deprecating laugh when she messed something up.

Soon he was remembering the touch of her hands on his back and shoulder, gently but persuasively massaging away his pain, her touch growing firmer with each session, forcing the blood flow around and into his injured tissues.

She always finished with the cords of his neck. His neck wasn't hurt. It didn't need the attention. But it was his favorite part of the massage.

It was intimate, reminding him of their lovemaking, which he was more than desperate to repeat. But he didn't dare ask her. She'd made the boundaries clear, and he had to respect that. Especially since it felt like she'd almost single-handedly cured him.

Jayden whinnied and shook his head, and Dallas saw they'd made it to the lake.

He dismounted, leading the horse for a drink, plunking himself down on the shore. The colored pebbles of the beach gave a little beneath him. He chose a large stone and tossed it far into the lake. It splashed, forming rings in the still water.

He threw another, then another.

As his arm grew tired, Sierra's image came back.

This time she was in his arms, her beautiful, smiling face above him, her long hair brushing his bare chest as they rocked together while making love.

"You're healing," she'd said to him then, and he'd thought about it many times since. It was more than just her hands. She had the power to touch him to his soul.

She'd leave soon, he knew. She'd been here more than a month already. She worked hard, but it was easy to see her heart wasn't in it. She didn't love the ranch the way a person, especially a woman, had to love the ranch to make a life on it.

He laughed at himself for even having that thought.

Who on earth would love sweeping stalls and cleaning tack all day long? It dawned on him then, like a bolt of lightning. They'd had her do the drudge work instead of experiencing the joy or fun of ranching.

He sat up straighter.

Why hadn't he thought of it before now?

Sierra should learn to ride.

She might like riding. She liked horses, and horses liked her.

He could offer to teach her. He *would* offer to teach her.

He came to his feet and shoved his hat on his head, intent on heading home to do just that.

Feeling lighter than he had in a very long time, he gathered Jayden's reins. It was still his birthday, and he was still home on the ranch, but as he stuffed his foot in the stirrup, he actually smiled.

Ten

In a pair of dove gray pajama pants and a pink kitten-paw T-shirt, Sierra pulled back the covers for an early night when a knock on the door stopped her.

"Just a sec," she called out, crossing the cool floor on her bare feet.

The household was mostly still up with muted sounds coming from outside and from deeper in the staff quarters. The window in her room was open behind her, the scent of fresh hay swirling over the small bedside lamp that gave the room a golden glow.

It was her turn to help Mrs. Innish with breakfast tomorrow. That meant biscuits in the oven at five, pounds of bacon and sausage on the grill, oatmeal to put on the boil and Sierra's surprisingly popular fruit salad to cut up.

She opened the door to find Dallas.

He looked relaxed, even a little happy, and her heart lifted.

She'd worried about him after he rode away this afternoon. She'd helped many people through the loss of a parent, and she wished he'd been comfortable enough to reach out to her on such a distressing day.

"Hi," she said softly, hoping he might want to talk now.

He took in her outfit, looking puzzled by it.

"Early morning in the kitchen," she explained.

"Can we talk for a minute?"

Her heart lifted a little more. "Yes. Sure." She stepped back.

He walked in the room, and she closed the door behind him, completely ready for whatever was on his mind.

He was still dressed in riding gear. His hair was mussed, and dust was streaked in the crook of his neck. He looked like he'd dropped Jayden off in the barn and come directly to her room.

"Sit down," she offered gently, gesturing to the chair. She perched herself on the bed.

He settled, then gazed at her for a long minute.

"So?" she prompted, wanting him to start the conversation with whatever was on his mind.

"I was thinking—out there riding and thinking." A more serious faraway look crossed his face.

"Hmm?" she offered with an encouraging nod.

"You've been here for a while now."

She waited.

"You've worked hard." He tapped his fingers against his knee.

"Thank you."

"I mean it." He met her gaze.

"Okay." She didn't want to rush him, and she didn't want to inadvertently steer the conversation in the wrong direction.

He could take all the time he needed.

He leaned forward, eyes softening, tone going lower. "You're doing the drudge work."

"I expected that." She didn't love shoveling manure and sweeping up dirty straw, but there were plenty of things she'd found she liked about working with animals.

It was soul-soothing for starters. Horses didn't have an agenda. Well, maybe Cedric did. But it certainly wasn't a hidden agenda. He made his desire for massage abundantly clear.

"You should be having some fun," Dallas said.

"I am having *some* fun." She smiled at her own joke. "It's not all fun."

"I could teach you to ride."

His offer took her by surprise. She'd thought about riding. She couldn't exactly help it here in the middle of a working ranch where everyone over the age of five hopped on a horse at some point.

"Sure," she said, not about to hesitate over an opportunity to spend time with him.

For his good, of course. And to fulfill her promise to McKinney and earn her keep.

The fact that her chest tightened, her pulse jumped and her lips tingled at the thought of him was secondary. She had to keep ignoring those reactions and focus on her job.

"Yeah?" he asked.

She nodded. "I'd appreciate that."

He grinned then and came to his feet.

She stood too.

The small room forced them close together. She could see the flecks of amber in his brown eyes, the sexy stubble of his beard, the fullness of his parted lips. He smelled of fresh air and fertile earth, and she swayed his way.

"Sierra." His whisper sounded pained.

She knew how he felt. The air was thick with the special brand of energy between them. She knew she had to ignore it. And she would. She'd ignore it in just a minute.

She breathed in his scent.

He leaned toward her.

She raised her palms, pretending she wanted to stop him but laying them flat against his chest instead, absorbing the heat of his skin and the beat of his heart.

"We—" he began.

She knew what he meant. She knew they couldn't. As desperately as she wanted him, they didn't dare give in to the temptation all over again.

She looked up to agree and apologize.

But his lips brushed hers.

Desire weakened her knees, and she gripped handfuls of his shirt.

His arms went around her waist. He deepened the kiss, and she clung to his shoulders, reveling in wave after wave of desire rushing through her.

They were chest to chest, thigh to thigh, their kisses growing faster and more frantic.

She reached for the hem of her shirt, intent on peeling it off and finally feeling her skin against his.

But his broad hand surrounded hers, holding them still. His kisses turned softer, and he drew back, his breathing ragged.

"I can't believe I'm saying this," he rasped, the hand around hers giving a squeeze.

"Saying what?" But she knew. She knew he was backing off, and regret flowed coldly over her skin.

His voice was a whisper. "You seemed to regret it last time."

She had. And she hadn't. But she had.

She gave a jerky little nod. She couldn't fault him for being a gentleman.

"I didn't come here for this," he said.

"I know you didn't." She dared to look him in the eyes. "You came to offer me riding lessons."

"The offer still stands."

"Thank you." She was glad now that he'd stopped, grateful he'd had the strength she wouldn't have been able to muster.

He slipped his hands away from her and stepped back. "Let me know when you have time."

"You let me know," she countered.

His schedule was busier than hers. And hers was fake anyway. Nobody would miss her if she wasn't sweeping the barn.

"Tomorrow?"

She nodded.

He stepped for the door and reached for the handle. "Good night, Sierra."

"Good night, Dallas." She tried to keep the desire out of her eyes, the regret and the wanting. But she suspected she failed.

He gazed at her a moment longer, the same regret filling his eyes. Then he opened the door and was gone.

Sierra sat down on the bed and, shaking, dropped her chin to her chest.

"Wow," she whispered under her breath. "Oh, wow."

How could passion possibly be that intense? He was a sexy cowboy, sure. But the ranch was chockablock with rugged good-looking cowboys. None of them even attracted her, never mind affected her like Dallas did.

How was she going to sleep with this arousal buzzing through her?

A soft knock on her door had her head whipping up.

She blinked and stared at the door, hardly believing it could be happening.

The knock sounded again.

Yes, her mind cried out. *Yes.*

She hopped to her feet and all but sprinted the few steps, pulling open the door with a ridiculous smile on her face.

McKinney stood there. She'd been away from the ranch for several days but was obviously back.

Sierra stepped away in shock, bracing herself with the doorknob.

"I hope you don't mind," McKinney said, entering the room.

"Uh—" Sierra couldn't stop herself from glancing up and down the hall. It was empty.

"Shifting the herd from the springs to the river cut was brutal. The only upside was the extra pizza I earned for the effort. Calories in and calories out works in your favor sometimes." McKinney sprawled in the chair.

Unlike Dallas, she looked like she'd recently showered and was wearing clean jeans and a soft flannel shirt.

Not that sweaty cowboy wasn't sexy. It had seemed off-the-charts sexy a few minutes ago.

Sierra shut the door.

McKinney kept talking. "Rudy and I took a run down to Glenwood Springs after. Pearl's Pizza is to die for if you ever get down there. We ended up staying a couple of nights, hitting every tack shop within a hundred miles. You can't pry that man away from leather goods." She laughed. "Anyway. I saw Dallas."

Sierra's senses sharpened. "Just now?"

Had McKinney seen Dallas sneaking out of Sierra's room? Okay, not sneaking. He'd been there for a legitimate purpose, and nothing had really happened between them.

Still, if McKinney asked, Sierra was going to come clean.

But McKinney was shaking her head. "When I first got

home. He was on his way back to the barn with Jayden."
She sat forward in the chair. "He was *smiling*."

"That's good."

"It's his *birthday*."

"I know. You told me about it." Sierra and McKinney
had talked after Dallas first revealed that his mother was
killed on his birthday.

"*Smiling*, Sierra."

Sierra focused on the good news. "That's really good.
That's progress."

"That's amazing. I don't know what you're doing."
McKinney waved her hands across in front of her. "I'm not
asking. I know you can't talk about your clients. So, don't
tell me anything you shouldn't. But…way to go, Sierra."

Sierra sat down on the edge of the bed. She couldn't
take credit for any big breakthrough. She and Dallas had
barely scratched the surface of what made him tick.

"I didn't do much," she said.

"Whatever it is you're doing, just keep doing it."

Sierra opened her mouth, but she was seriously conflicted here.

McKinney grinned widely. "I'm so glad you're here."

"So am I," Sierra said honestly.

McKinney's expression turned serious. "So, it's helping? For you too? Being here is helping?"

"It's helping." Sierra barely even thought about Roger
anymore.

She was glad now that they'd split up. She'd felt that way
for weeks. If she was honest with herself, she'd known it
for sure after Dallas's first kiss.

If she could kiss another man like that. If she could
feel that way about kissing—a way she'd never felt kissing Roger—then she and Roger wouldn't have made it in

the long run. He was the wrong man for her, and she was lucky the marriage never happened.

"Good," McKinney said with a sharp nod, coming to her feet. "I'll get out of your hair. It looks like you're heading for bed."

"Breakfast duty with Mrs. Innish."

McKinney hesitated. "You sure that's okay? I didn't bring you here to work in the kitchen."

"I don't mind a little cooking. My fruit salad is a hit."

"With the cowboys?"

"Imagine."

McKinney left on a laugh, and Sierra leaned back against the closed door. She took a deep breath and let her shoulders slump in foolish disappointment over Dallas's strength of character.

A knock on the panel behind her made her jump.

She schooled her features and twisted the knob, wondering what McKinney had forgotten.

She opened the door to Dallas.

He was back.

In seconds he was pushing the door shut behind himself and she was welcoming him into her arms.

With Sierra enfolded naked in his arms, Dallas savored the moment, kissing her sweet lips, her neck, her shoulder, inhaling the sweet scent of her hair.

He'd tried hard to stay away, acutely aware of her second thoughts the last time they'd made love. But a woman could change her mind. And it had seemed like Sierra might have changed hers. So, he'd knocked on her door to ask.

It was crowded now with both of them on her single bed, but he didn't care. He'd make love with her anytime, anywhere, any way. Heaven was her bare skin, her soft moans, her passionate kisses and her arms wrapped around his neck.

He was stronger than the last time, and he propped himself on his elbow, keeping his weight from her while he explored her breasts, the indentation of her waist, the flare of her hips and the supple smooth skin of her thighs.

"You soothe me," he whispered, feeling a deep-seated impulse to be honest.

"Massage does that," she answered between kisses, playfully pulling at his bottom lip, her hands beginning their own exploration of his nakedness.

"It's not the massage." While his body rose to her touch, he drew his spread fingers through her loose hair, drawing it back from her face and looking into her eyes. "It's—I don't know—what you say, what you do, the sound of your voice and the beauty of your smile."

She treated him to that wonderful smile.

"And your eyes," he said. "You have amazing, amazing eyes."

"That's your hormones talking."

"I don't mean sex." He was obviously saying this wrong. He didn't want to say this wrong. He desperately wanted to get it right.

"Endorphins, maybe even enkephalins," she added on a sigh, as if the words were sexy talk. Then she kissed him deeply again. "Who knows what invisible elements might be impacting you."

"You know I don't believe in all that."

"You don't have to believe in it. Pheromones will get you either way." Her exploration became more intimate, sending a white-hot surge of passion into his brain.

He tried to say more, but it came out as a groan.

"Dallas," she whispered.

He captured her mouth in a deep, deep kiss.

She moaned and shifted beneath him, wrapping a leg around his hips.

He settled closer still, his heartbeat deepening and quickening in anticipation.

She flexed her hips, and he rocked into her.

"Yes," she hissed in his ear. "Oh, yes."

Her enthusiasm spurred him forward, and he thrust against her, kissing her mouth, palming her breasts, letting her breathlessness and small moans set his pace. He was desperate to have this last as long as it could. He'd go forever if that were possible.

The breeze cooled his back. But the scent of the raw outdoors faded as he inhaled Sierra, tasted Sierra, felt the heat of her body wrapped around him and reveled in every passing second.

The seconds stretched to minutes, the pleasure going on and on and on.

But it was still too soon when she cried out, her body tightening, hijacking what remained of his senses and sending him rocketing to the stars.

He frantically drew in oxygen, kissing her neck and shoulders as his breathing recovered.

Her own rapid breaths puffed in his ear.

Their heartbeats synced where their chests were pressed together.

He worried he was crushing her and tried to move off.

But she tightened her arms around him. "Not yet."

"You sure?"

She nodded against his hair. "I don't want to come back to earth."

"I'm with you on that." Euphoria was still circulating through him. He didn't particularly care what hormonal cocktail had caused it. He'd hang on to it until the end.

He'd never made love like this. He'd never felt like this.

He'd never held a woman in his arms after lovemaking and tried to figure out a way to not let her go.

His breathing steadied, and his heart rate slowed.

The sounds of outside filtered into his ears: the burble of the creek, the frogs' chorus and the whinny of a horse far away in the paddock.

"Well," Sierra said.

He didn't know what she meant.

"This is quite a predicament," she added.

He eased to the side, keeping an arm around her, pushing stray locks of hair from her flushed face so he could see her better. He sure wasn't seeing a predicament here.

"How so?" he asked.

"I feel like I need to tell McKinney."

The words surprised Dallas since Sierra had seemed intent on keeping their relationship discreet. He was fine with whatever she wanted. He'd be happy to shout it from the rooftop.

He was just surprised by her apparent change of heart. "Why would you need to tell anyone?"

Sierra hesitated, worry flitting across her pretty blue eyes. "Because we're friends."

"And?" To Dallas's mind, Sierra was still entitled to her privacy.

She bit down her bottom lip. "And I don't want to keep such a big secret."

It occurred to him that telling McKinney might mean Sierra wanted to openly—

His thought process stopped there. To openly what? Sleep with him? Date him?

Was it possible Sierra had feelings for him? He knew he had feelings for her, and they were turning serious. They were growing stronger by the day, maybe by the hour.

"Up to you," he said in a causal tone. What he really wanted to do was shout *yes*!

"But then—" Sierra shifted onto her side as she spoke, propping up on one elbow to face him "—I'd be asking her to keep a secret from the rest of the family. And that's not fair. And if she told them—then—you know."

"I know what?" He couldn't figure out what she was talking about. And he didn't think McKinney would share Sierra and his personal life with anyone else.

"It would be awkward, me working for you."

"Not so awkward." He kissed her hairline. It was nobody else's businesses, and he wouldn't let them stick their noses in.

She closed her eyes, and her voice dropped to a whisper. "What a mess. I've made such a mess."

"You haven't done anything wrong." He hated that she was feeling bad. He was feeling fantastic. He wanted to make love with her again. He wanted to drift off to sleep with her.

Well, maybe not *here*. His bed would be much preferable. He was close to falling off the edge of the narrow mattress right now.

"You should leave," she said, looking quite miserable. "Forget this ever happened. Go back to the way we were."

He heaved a sigh. "Are we going to go round and round on this again? We don't seem to be able to stay away from each other."

"We can't have a secret affair."

"Are you married? No. Engaged? No. I'm not married, and I'm not engaged. I'm not involved with anyone either."

"I hope not," she said, her brow furrowing.

"My point is, it's not an affair. Neither of us is cheating on anyone."

Sierra flattened her lips. "I'm cheating on McKinney."

He couldn't help but chuckle at that. "You're not dating McKinney."

"I have an obligation to her."

"As her friend?"

Sierra nodded. "Would you mind, Dallas? If we backed off? At least while I think this through?"

"I'd mind very, very much," he said softly. "But it's your call, Sierra. Nothing happens between us that you don't want to happen. Tell McKinney. Don't tell McKinney. But I'm still going to teach you to ride."

She gazed at him for a long moment, and he was sure she was going to refuse the riding lessons. He'd argue back, and he'd make her see reason. He wasn't leaving without a yes on that at least. The woman deserved to experience the fun side of ranching.

"Outside," she said instead. "In the daylight with other people watching."

"You can have as big an audience as you want."

She nodded to that. Her eyes turned soft seafoam blue, a sadness clouding them. "I don't trust us."

Desire swelled up in his chest all over again. He kissed her swollen lips. "I don't trust us either. You're under my skin, Sierra. I'll keep my hands to myself, but I won't like it."

"Dallas," she said in a warning tone.

"I'm going to miss you the second I leave your bed."

She smiled a little sadly at his words. "I'll miss you too. I'd be lying to say I wouldn't."

"Thanks for being honest."

She smiled again and shook her head, a touch of light coming back into her eyes. "Oh, man. We're really messed up here."

He touched the bottom of her chin, tipping her face up to his. "I don't regret a single second. You shouldn't either."

"Good night, Dallas," she said in a tone of resignation.

"Good night, sweet Sierra. I'll find you tomorrow." He rose from the bed and shrugged into his clothes. He paused then, long enough to lock the image of her in his mind before slipping out the bedroom door.

Dallas had been creative.

Sierra would give him that.

She'd asked him to make sure her riding lessons happened in broad daylight with people watching, and he'd more than respected her wishes. It was midafternoon in the bright sunshine with clouds forming a fringe in the mountains above them.

"Look at me!" Zeke called out, turning his compact horse in a zigzag pattern around the orange pylons set up in a long line across the corral.

"I'm faster," Albert returned, getting ready to start his own turn.

"Don't you try to go fast," Dallas said to Sierra from where he was mounted beside her.

She was astride a docile dapple-gray mare named Frothy who was eleven years old with a sweet disposition. Sierra had adopted a battered tan Stetson from McKinney several weeks back, and it kept the hot sun from her face.

There wasn't much to be done about the dust in her eyes. But she was getting used to taking shallow breaths when a cloud of it came up.

At a distance, Cedric was whinnying at the paddock fence, sounding offended that Sierra was cavorting with another horse.

"I have no intention of going fast," she assured Dallas.

"Gentle on the rein." He demonstrated again as Albert finished his run. "Pay attention to your posture and look where you're going. Horses respond to your body position. If you look left, they want to go left."

"Got it," she answered, cataloging all the instructions in her mind.

"Give her a kick," Dallas said.

Sierra gently tapped her heels, and Frothy started for the beginning of the pylon course.

Albert and Zeke stayed well out of the way while they watched. It was clear they'd had riding lessons before and knew the etiquette.

Cedric, on the other hand, continued to kick up a fuss.

Frothy also knew the drill. With barely any instructions from Sierra, the horse moved perfectly through the line of orange traffic cones.

"Nicely done," Dallas said approvingly as she came back to him.

"It wasn't me."

"Sure, it was you."

Sierra patted Frothy on the neck. "This one knows exactly what she's doing."

"I wasn't going to put you on a half-trained horse."

Sierra eyed him up suspiciously as Zeke and Albert restarted the exercise. "You gave me the expert horse."

"I did want you to succeed," he said sheepishly.

"You use her for the five-year-old children, don't you?"

He grinned. "Guilty as charged."

"I don't know whether to be insulted or grateful."

"I want you to enjoy yourself." He raised his voice so Zeke and Albert could hear. "Shall we finish with a trail ride?"

"Trail ride," Zeke called out.

"Yes!" Albert said, punching his fist in the air.

"You up for it?" Dallas asked Sierra. "Butt getting too sore?"

"My butt is fine." It wasn't perfect, but it wasn't overly sore either. She recalled from her long-ago riding weekend with McKinney that a certain amount of discomfort was inevitable when people were new on a horse.

"Remember what I said, try to go with the motion of the horse." He started forward.

Sierra didn't quite understand how to move with the horse, but she was determined to try. She nudged Frothy, who seemed to understand that her job was to follow Jayden.

"Where're we going?" Albert asked while he opened the gate from the back of his horse.

Cedric's whinnies grew almost frantic as he pranced back and forth along the fence line watching them.

"Up to the green pond," Dallas called out. "Don't get too far ahead." He looked Cedric's way, gave his head a shake and adjusted his Stetson. "Zeke, go get Cedric. He can come along."

Sierra's heart warmed with Dallas's compassionate gesture. But she was confused. "Doesn't he need a rider?"

Dallas turned back with a crinkle-eyed grin. "You think he might leave you?"

"I don't know." If a horse was set free, might it not just go wherever it wanted? If Cedric ran into the hills, how would they get him back?

"He's like a big ole dog where it comes to you."

Zeke's mount was trotting to a gate in the paddock fence while the rest of them waited in place.

"If you say so." Sierra knew Dallas was the expert, but if horses were so predictable, why pen them up in the first place? And every cowboy on the Hawkes ranch was absolutely meticulous about gates and fences. She'd observed that from day one.

As soon as the gate was open, Cedric charged through it, thundering in a beeline toward Sierra.

She reflexively drew back as a whole lot of determined and possibly angry horse bore down on them.

"Look out," she said to Albert, shooing him off to the side.

Although she was the obvious target, she was hoping Dallas would intervene somehow and slow Cedric down before he got there.

"Why?" Albert asked her.

"I think he's mad," Sierra said.

Frothy sidestepped beneath her.

"Relax," Dallas said, moving in front of Cedric's path. "He's just a little jealous."

"Frothy's worried," Sierra pointed out. The horse was still shifting beneath her.

"She's taking her cues from you." As Dallas spoke, Cedric slowed down.

"There you go," Dallas said, backing his horse up to give Frothy some more space.

Cedric slowed to a stop, shook his head, then nodded and whinnied happily. He sidled around beside Frothy, who didn't seem to mind, and stretched his neck out, inviting Sierra to lean over and pet him.

She did.

"Let's go," Albert called happily, and the two boys trotted toward a fringe of woods.

There was room on the trail for Sierra and Dallas to ride side by side, and Cedric settled happily in behind Frothy. It was quiet in the trees. Clouds were meeting above them now, blocking out the afternoon sun, bringing welcome bursts of cooler air.

Dallas seemed relaxed and in his element on the trail.

"What do you think?" he asked her.

"I think it's going to take me a while to learn." She shifted in the saddle, her butt feeling the pinch now. But she didn't want to complain.

"And the rest of the ranch?" He kept his attention on the trail as he asked the question. "What are your impressions of living here?"

It struck her as odd that he wasn't looking her way as he asked. But then she remembered his instruction to look where she wanted the horse to go. He was simply showing good riding habits.

She looked ahead while she answered. "I like it." She did.

When she agreed to come, she'd hoped the ranch would be a calm, quiet spot where she could get her head together. It was. What she hadn't expected was her affinity with Cedric and the rest of the horses. She hadn't expected the wide-open spaces to feel so freeing. And she sure hadn't expected Dallas.

Dallas. She squeezed her eyes shut for a second as emotion welled up inside her. Last night in his arms had been magic. He was tender and selfless, intuitive, even funny. For a man wrapped up in his personal pain, he'd shown an astonishing level of empathy.

"Care to elaborate?" he asked.

She slid him a glance, trying to decide if he was fishing for something. "Are you asking about last night?"

"No. Not at all." He spread an arm expansively around them. "I'm asking about the ranch. As a city girl?"

She didn't know whether to be relieved or disappointed. One side of her wanted to relive last night with him, marvel together at what had happened between them. But the wiser, more reasonable side knew it was important to push past that experience and focus on Dallas's psyche.

"As a city girl, I like the ranch. I like the horses."

Cedric whinnied from behind as if he understood.

Dallas chuckled. "And they like you."

"I like the space." She paused to put her words into thoughts. "I thought I'd be intimidated by it, miles and miles of rugged nothing in every direction. But it's oddly soothing. I can see why you love it here." She cracked the door open for him to either agree or disagree with that statement. She was expecting him to disagree.

"It's not for everyone," he said.

"It's paradise for some." She paused to let him respond, watching closely to decipher the micro-expressions crossing his face.

"I'm glad you feel that way." He looked genuinely happy, but he kept his own opinion to himself.

"It's a place to build a good life, Dallas." She tried prodding one more time, hoping he was coming to understand the truth of that. Sure, he had some bad memories. But everybody had bad memories. He also had a family here—a family who loved and cared about him and desperately wanted him to stay.

"You think?" he asked, looking thoughtful now.

"I know it." She dared to go a bit further. "You're a lucky man."

He gave a half smile and a half laugh at that. "Some days I feel luckier than others."

Eleven

Austin plunked himself into an Adirondack chair next to Dallas.

It was late, and the wood fire had burned down to coals in the patio firepit. A shimmering heat wave rose from the orange embers too hot to form smoke.

Austin's breathing was chopped, his words edged with frustration. "I just don't get what you're going to do."

"About what?" Dallas had been thinking about Sierra.

She was a complication in his life, a fascinating complication. Like a finely bred bronco, she twisted him into a knot, tossed him high and left him dizzy and floundering in midair.

He didn't have the slightest idea what he was going to do about her.

"Don't get cute," Austin said. He rose and tossed a log on the fire, sending a shower of sparks toward the black sky before sitting down hard.

Dallas leaned an arm against the slatted back of the

chair and twisted to face his brother. "I've never once been cute."

Austin's gaze sharpened. His lips pursed as he impatiently waited.

Dallas lifted his brow in a silent question.

"About the *land*," Austin spat out.

"Oh, that." Dallas had some thoughts on that. They were half-formed and fuzzy. But he had been thinking about what the new deed meant for his future.

"Give me a break," Austin muttered.

"I don't know."

"I don't believe you."

"I've known about it for all of—what—five days?"

"You're not the only person impacted."

"I know that."

His father had made no secret of wanting Dallas to throw in his lot with his siblings and create the family dynasty his grandfather had imagined all those years ago.

Austin wanted to make cattle ranching as easy and efficient as possible—to run the entire operation from behind a computer terminal with a series of satellite links and a swarm of drones. But what was even the point of that? What was the point of ranching without the hard work and risk that made a man concentrate, sweat all day, then sleep soundly at night?

Dallas wanted the rodeo again. He wanted to be on the road, to share in the action and excitement to keep his mind and body too busy for regret.

He knew his shoulder might not get back the range of motion it needed to compete at the highest level. The years might be catching up with him. And he might not be sure he wanted to heal from another injury like this.

But he wasn't ready to sit behind a desk either. And he couldn't spend his days in full view of the road where his mother had died, across the meadow from her tombstone, living in the rooms where she'd loved and laughed and embraced her life.

He'd had the best mother in the world.

"You say that," Austin responded. "But I don't think you get it."

"You think I'm incapable of basic reasoning?"

"Have you thought it through?"

"The family dynasty versus cash in my pocket? That kind of thought it through?" .

"You'd sell? You'd actually sell?"

"Tell me you didn't think about it when you got yours."

Austin frowned in disgust. "For about half a second. Do you know what we've got here? Do you have any idea what guys would do to have the opportunity we have? This land?" He pointed back and forth between himself and Dallas. "This *us*?"

"Us?" Dallas didn't feel like part of a team.

"Yes, us. There are four of us. Dad was completely alone when he took over. He hung on to this place through sheer guts and hard work, so we'd have a chance with it."

"Tyler is halfway around the world. My life is—" Dallas gestured down the road toward the highway. "Out there. And who knows what McKinney will decide to do."

"McKinney loves this land."

"McKinney will love someone else one day. And who knows what he'll want. Look at Ethan Douglas."

Austin's nostrils flared and he squared his shoulders. "You think there's something going on between Ethan and McKinney?"

"I meant she might not fall in love with a rancher."

"But not Ethan."

"No, not Ethan. At least not that I've ever seen."

Austin seemed to relax. He nodded. "Okay."

"You got something against Ethan?"

"I barely know him. But he's—" Austin grimaced. "Kind of techy."

"You like techy."

"McKinney won't be happy in a city."

Dallas nodded. He had to agree with Austin on that.

He agreed with Austin on plenty of things. In fact, Austin was usually right about the big picture. He mostly gave good advice. In fact, looking back, the biggest mistakes Dallas had made in his life were when through sheer bullheadedness he'd ignored his older brother.

It was a sobering thought.

"You remember New Year's Eve when the Krebb brothers built that still?" Dallas asked.

Austin cracked a smile. "I think I still have a headache from their moonshine."

Dallas empathized. They'd been teenagers at the time, too young to buy whiskey. Neighbors Pete and Stanford Krebb had been industrious if nothing else.

"Stormy wanted to set off fireworks," Dallas continued with his main point.

"That guy always had wild ideas."

"All we had was dynamite."

"I remember."

"You stopped me."

Austin looked puzzled.

"I was going to help Stormy with the dynamite, and you stopped me. I cussed you out something fierce, but you pinned me against the barn wall and told me I was acting like a fool."

"You *were*," Austin said emphatically.

"I *know*."

The two men went silent for a moment, the fire log crackling away beside them, radiating heat and yellow light.

"Your point?" Austin finally asked.

"No real point. You were right. Stormy lost a finger that night."

"Hasn't seemed to much miss it."

Dallas gave a low chuckle. "I suppose not."

Stormy still worked on the Hawkes ranch. He might not be the most brilliant ranch hand, but he was tough as nails and harder working than most.

Dallas came to his feet. "I am thinking."

"Yeah?"

"I do know it's not just about me."

Austin rose. "You don't have to leave."

"I don't see how I stay." Dallas's mind seized up in something like panic whenever he contemplated staying.

"Mom's death was an accident."

"I know." It was right there on the sheriff's report.

"You couldn't have stopped her."

Dallas pasted his brother with a look of disbelief. "We both know I could have."

"You wouldn't have found her."

"I should have tried."

"Maybe," Austin allowed. "Who knew where she went in town that night. We'll never know why she stayed so late into the storm."

"The town isn't that big." Dallas would have checked everywhere—the restaurants, her friends' houses. If he'd left when Austin first told him to go, he knew he could have tracked her down before she drove home alone.

It was a moment before Austin spoke again. "We need to think about the future, not the past."

"Yeah, sure." Dallas brushed off the trite words.

"You don't think there was guilt to go around when Uncle Richmond died? Every cowboy on that drive, including Dad must have—"

"Dad was a teenager," Dallas interjected.

"What do you think you were?"

"Eighteen's different than fourteen. By a long shot."

"I'm just saying—"

"I *know* you want me to stay." Dallas's frustration grew along with the edge in his tone. "I know it. I'm thinking about it. I'm working stuff out. *Okay?*"

Austin hesitated, then gave a short nod.

"Good." Dallas was suddenly tired. He was bone-tired, and his shoulder was aggravatingly sore.

He wanted Sierra. No, he needed Sierra.

He wondered where she was right now.

Sierra was stepping in on kitchen duty for another staff member. A housecleaner, Belinda, had gone into town last night for her sister's birthday.

"You're a kind soul to take her turn," Mrs. Innish said as she mixed biscuit dough in a large steel bowl. Flour speckled her cheek and had dusted the front of her red apron.

"It was a birthday party," Sierra answered. "I hope she had a good time."

"Hmph. Grown-ups don't need cakes and candles and silly hats."

"Grown-ups still need to have fun." It was important for everyone to let loose and celebrate the happy things in life. "A birthday is just a good excuse. Belinda works hard."

"We all work hard."

Sierra regretted how she'd phrased that. "I know you work harder than most."

Mrs. Innish's tone was tart. "Everyone has a certain lot in life. People need to accept theirs."

It made Sierra sad to hear that sentiment. "You don't think people can improve their own lives?"

Mrs. Innish retrieved a rolling pin and floured her wooden board. "They can try."

Sierra sliced her way through a line of ripe melons for the fruit salad. "We all should try." She knew everyone had strengths, and everyone had opportunities. It was a matter of finding your own and doing your best with them.

"But not too hard." There was an odd tone to Mrs. Innish's voice.

Sierra was intrigued. "What do you mean?"

Mrs. Innish gave her a long, measured look.

Sierra grew uncomfortable. "What?"

"You know what happens." Mrs. Innish paused. "To staff members around here who get too close to the family."

Sierra realized Mrs. Innish was talking about her son Raymond again. She didn't want to get into that topic, so she turned to a crate of apples and took her time selecting a few.

"They're going to figure it out soon," Mrs. Innish said from behind her.

"Hmm," Sierra answered vaguely. She turned on the faucet in the island sink, concentrating on washing the apples.

"McKinney might not know what's going on yet, but Dallas is sure as shootin' going to give it away."

Sierra nearly dropped an apple as the words penetrated.

"I see how he looks at you." Mrs. Innish's voice was laced with self-satisfaction. "And I see how you look back. I don't know what happens when you two—"

"*Excuse* me." Sierra cut the woman off.

Mrs. Innish had the grace to look guilty. "All's I'm saying, is watch yourself. McKinney obviously likes you. But the Hawkes don't take kindly to fraternization. And I doubt they take kindly to secrets."

Sierra realized the water was still running cold over her

hands. She quickly shut off the tap and sorted the apples onto the cutting board in front of her, a kind of panic curling in her stomach.

If Mrs. Innish saw something between her and Dallas, who else could see it?

"I like you, Sierra," Mrs. Innish said kindly. "I can be an old gossip, I know. But gossip is a part of life, especially in a place like this. You need to decide. What it is you really want and if it's worth the potential fallout."

It was hard to be annoyed with Mrs. Innish since she was only being honest.

Sierra nodded.

Her situation might be vastly different from Mrs. Innish's son. But Sierra was keeping a dangerous secret from McKinney. She was failing in her professional obligation to Dallas, and she had to come clean.

"I figured as much." Mrs. Innish pressed her metal biscuit cutter into the dough over and over again. "Don't let him trifle with you. Think about yourself and your future here."

Sierra had to fight a smile at the word *trifle*. She was hardly a fair maiden whose virtue was at stake. In fact, she was the one doing Dallas wrong, not the other way around.

"I will," Sierra promised. "And thank you."

Mrs. Innish looked puzzled.

"For being honest with me. I appreciate it."

"Okay. Well, then." Mrs. Innish seemed flustered by Sierra's response. She glanced at the clock. "We need to get a move on. We're running behind."

Sierra managed to avoid Dallas for the rest of the day, then tracked McKinney down in the early evening near the barn where she was brushing her horse. The setting sun left hints of orange and pink across the clouds while the dome of the sky darkened to indigo.

"Have a good day with the cows?" Sierra asked as she made her way across the soft dirt of the runout pen.

McKinney grinned over her shoulder, excitement in her voice as she started to talk. "It was good fun. We were up the south valley with the home herd. Ethan's testing out a new microchip system. You should see the thing. It uses ear tags and wand readers, all connected to GPS and a central database."

"Impressive." Sierra had listened to Ethan often enough to know he and Austin had far-reaching plans for modernizing cattle management.

"How about you?" McKinney asked, firmly stroking the horse's flank with a stiff brush and raising dust with the effort. "Anything happen on the home front?"

"Not too much." Now that she had McKinney alone, Sierra hesitated.

"Did you get a chance to see Dallas?"

"Not today. I was in the barn, and he was—you know—out and about."

McKinney nodded. "Can't win 'em all, I guess. Have you had dinner? I'll have to forage in the kitchen by the time I get showered. You should meet me there. We can chow down and have something to drink."

"Sure." Sierra was relieved by the thought of putting off the conversation.

On the other hand, if they talked in the main house someone might interrupt, maybe even Dallas.

"Great." McKinney dropped the brush into a wooden carrying crate. She untied the horse's lead rope from the fence rail.

The sunset had faded now, and the yard lights were coming on.

"McKinney, wait."

McKinney paused and turned, looking puzzled by the tone in Sierra's voice. "Yeah? Something up?"

"Yes. Something's up."

McKinney took a step closer, peering worriedly at Sierra. "You okay?"

"I'm fine. Physically." Emotionally was another matter.

"Good. Did you hear from Roger or something?"

Sierra shook her head, telling herself to spit it out already. "No. Nothing from him." He wasn't even on her mind these days. "It's Dallas."

McKinney's brow furrowed with concern. "I thought you didn't see him today."

"I didn't. It wasn't today."

McKinney cocked her head. "He seemed okay last time I saw him. Yesterday, I think. It was in the morning. You guys were going to do riding lessons. Wait. How did that go? Did something happen? Was he a jerk?"

"No." Sierra shook her head more vigorously. "Him and me—that is—we—"

"You're not going to quit on me, are you?" McKinney moved closer still, while her horse stood patiently waiting. "Please tell me you're not going to quit."

"I'm not going to quit."

"Oh, thank goodness."

"But you might want to fire me."

McKinney chuckled like Sierra was making a joke. "Why would you even say that?"

"Because I slept with Dallas." There. Sierra had finally spit it out. It was a relief.

McKinney's expression froze for a moment. "You *what*?" It was impossible to tell if she was angry or shocked.

"I'm sorry."

"Wait. Go back. Start over. What the heck?"

"There was an attraction—between us."

"You *think*?"

Sierra scrambled to explain. "I backed way off after we first kissed. I figured I could handle it. I mean, I'm a professional, right?" Sierra didn't feel much like a professional right now. "But it got stronger. And then we were alone."

"When? Where? How?" McKinney waved her hand in front of her like she was erasing the words. "Okay, forget how. I don't need to know how."

"Downstairs in the gym. I was giving him a massage. Looking back, that was a really bad idea."

"He said the massages worked wonders."

"They did. They usually do. But it was late at night. Nobody was around. And, well, you can guess the rest."

"Wow." McKinney blew out a breath.

"I'm so sorry I lied."

"You didn't lie. It's not like I asked you if you'd had sex with my brother."

"I should have owned up to it right away. I should never have tried to work with him as a client once I knew we couldn't keep our hands off each other."

McKinney stifled a grin. "He's not exactly an ordinary client."

"Not anymore."

"He never was. This was a stealth operation. You were more a friend than a coach."

"I think that makes it worse." It was secrets on top of secrets. Sierra knew that wasn't healthy for any of them. The magnitude of what she'd done was beginning to sink in. "I should go."

"What? No. You can't leave. He's so much better now."

"And that's good." Sierra would admit Dallas had come a long way, both physically and emotionally. But she couldn't continue working with him under these circumstances. It wasn't fair to him.

"Are you still—" McKinney paused meaningfully.

"No. It only happened twice."

McKinney looked amused. "Twice?"

"It would be so much more dignified to be able to say once, wouldn't it?"

"Like you slipped, but then realized the error of your ways and virtuously stopped yourself?"

"Exactly."

"Still, twice isn't bad. You've been here over a month. Twice is really pretty good, don't you think?"

Considering how often she'd dreamed of making love with Dallas, twice felt pretty good to Sierra—like she'd exhibited enormous self-control.

"It's not like you're in a relationship with him," McKinney continued.

"I can't coach him anymore." Sierra was clear on that now, even if she'd deluded herself for a while.

"You don't have to coach him, per se. Just hang around a bit longer. Chat with him some more." McKinney gave a shrug. "Even sleep with him if you want to since you're not his coach."

"I can't be intimate with him without being honest with him."

McKinney drew back, her eyes going wide. "Oh, you can't do that."

"It feels like I should."

McKinney vigorously shook her head. "That would be the death of both of us. He's in a good place right now, Sierra. Thanks to you, he's feeling way better than he was before. I've seen him smile at dinner. He even joked with Victor. We don't dare mess that up."

"Then I have to leave." Sierra's chest hurt as she said the words.

"A few more days?" McKinney pleaded. "Maybe pick a date, give a slow, graceful goodbye, nothing too sudden, nothing too shocking so nobody gets upset or suspicious. Plus, it'll give you some time to find the right situation in California. Maybe with Nancy in LA?"

Sierra hated to agree because a long goodbye with Dallas would be so painful. But she could see it would be best for him. She owed him that much at least.

And McKinney was right. If Sierra left the ranch, she'd have to go somewhere. It would take a few days at least to set something up.

"Okay," she said.

McKinney heaved a sigh of relief. "Good. Thanks. Oh, man, I'm going to miss you."

"I'm going to miss you too." Sierra blinked back a sudden stinging sensation. There was so much about the Hawkes ranch she would miss.

Sierra had the perfect opportunity right now to tell Dallas she was leaving.

He'd taken the riding class on a field trip today. With ranch hand Hardy Rawlings's help, they'd trailered the horses to the northwest corner of the ranch and done a short trail ride to the White Foam Falls.

It was a picturesque setting, a high plateau rolling into a westward pass between the peaks that fed the dramatic waterfall and the deep, green pool below it.

Albert and Zeke were swimming now, shrieking in the cold water under Hardy's watchful eye.

Sierra sat with Dallas on a blanket spread out in the meadow thirty feet above the pool. They'd watered and picketed the horses, then ate a makeshift picnic of fruit and granola bars, before the boys spotted a pair of jackrabbits and tried to stealthily creep up for a better look.

The jackrabbits were wary, and quickly disappeared into a willow thicket.

"This is a beautiful spot," Sierra said, kicking herself for the banal observation when she had more important things to say.

The boys wouldn't keep swimming forever, so she had to spit it out.

"One of my favorites," Dallas answered. He was sprawled back on his elbows, while she was sitting with her legs curled beneath herself. It was beyond tempting to stretch out beside him and rest her head on his shoulder.

He pointed to the north side of the pond where the meadow stretched into the flatter highlands. "I can picture a house right there in the middle of all that graze."

"You would see graze? I can't believe you'd let the cattle mess up all those lovely wildflowers."

Still, it warmed her heart to hear him thinking about staying home on the ranch. Of all the progress they'd made, this was by far the most significant.

"Horses," he said. "Not cattle."

"Oh. Well, I guess that's prettier."

"Log walls for the house," he continued. "But no stone. Peaked roofs to shed the snow. Windows and ceiling beams, I think. But nothing too huge."

"You don't like the family mansion?"

"Do you?"

The big house was gorgeous, there was no doubt of that. But it didn't have much of a family home feel to it.

"It's a bit like living in a hotel," she said.

"Exactly," he agreed.

She could barely believe he was talking about building a house right here on the ranch—even theoretically.

She pressed him a bit to see how far he was willing to go. "How many bedrooms?"

"I don't know. Four, maybe."

She wanted to ask if he was thinking about kids. But the question put a lump in her throat, and she couldn't speak.

"A deck and a patio," he said into the silence. Then he gestured with his hands. "The length of the front so it was south-facing. That way you can stretch out the grilling season."

She had no trouble picturing Dallas presiding over a grill of burgers or ribs or fish. "You like grilling?"

"Everything tastes better outside."

"I'll take your word for that."

"You don't like picnics?" He spread his arms out in disbelief.

"This was a terrific picnic."

He sobered and sat up. "You like it here?"

"I do." She nodded. "I like it a lot."

"You don't think it's too remote?"

It was quiet, that was for sure. But she didn't want to dissuade him from his emotionally healthy vision. "We're only a mile from the highway."

"True," he said thoughtfully. "It's only an hour into Jagged Creek. The road's better. In some ways, it's more convenient to town than the main homestead."

"That's a good point."

"Can you picture it?" he asked earnestly.

"A home right here?" she asked.

It was the easiest thing in the world to picture, and it was beautiful. She wanted to feel good about accomplishing this much for him. She wanted to be happy for McKinney and the whole family that Dallas had come so far. But the lump in her throat turned into a lead weight and dropped to her stomach as she realized her time with him was over.

She nodded.

A sublime smile lit up his brown eyes. "I was thinking about how to identify the horses."

She wondered if he meant the microchip ear tags.

"They'll be rodeo stock," he continued, his vision softening on the meadow beyond her. "Breed them, raise them, train them and make a name for myself." His enthusiasm ramped up as he spoke. "I could be out on the circuit without actually competing."

The stinging sensation came up behind her eyes at the image of his perfect life without her in it. It was hard to keep her voice from cracking. "That sounds perfect."

He nodded. "I know."

Silence rose between them as he seemed to picture his future.

She swallowed hard. "Dallas?"

"Hmm?"

She shook off her hesitation. She was making way too big a deal out of this. It wasn't some monumental, unexpected announcement. It was simply the next logical step.

"I'll be leaving in a few days."

His gaze flew her way, and he drew back in what looked like stupefaction.

"Maybe next week," she pushed on. "It's been great here. And I appreciate everything you've done for me. But, you know—"

"Leaving?" he echoed incredulously.

"I've been here longer than I'd planned already." That wasn't strictly true since she'd arrived without a timeline. But she'd stayed longer than she'd expected.

Still, she didn't want to leave. She was picturing herself in Dallas's ranch house in the meadow. Worse, she was picturing a couple of kids running around.

He leaned her way. "What are you even talking about? What is it you think we're doing here?"

"Planning your future." She came up on her knees to face him, mustering up her joy at all his progress. "And I'm so glad. You've come so far."

"And what about *your* future?"

She didn't have an immediate answer for that. "I'll figure that out."

"In California?" he asked on an unexpectedly bitter note.

"Probably." California held no appeal to her right now. But it was the logical choice. She had personal and professional connections in the state. She'd have job opportunities in any number of cities.

"Right," he said, coming to his feet. "Hey," he called down to Hardy and the boys. "Time to get a move on."

They looked startled by the interruption and the tense tone of Dallas's voice. But they all immediately scrambled to get going.

Dallas was certain he hadn't misread the signs.

Sierra hadn't been coy. She'd made no secret of the fact she was attracted to him. She'd wanted to be discreet. He respected that.

But even without the lovemaking, their past weeks together had been fantastic. She'd taken to horseback riding like a pro. She was fearless, determined and industrious, with an ability to laugh at her mistakes and learn from them.

He'd thought she was having a great time. Even better, he'd thought she was falling for him the way he was falling for her. And he was falling fast and hard for her.

The woman had stealthily and systemically sidelined his bad memories and laid new tracks. When he gazed over the range these past days, or into the mountains, or even down the road toward town and the gully where his mother had died, he saw Sierra. He saw her soft smile, heard her gentle laugh, knew her very presence soothed his emotional pain.

Now the pain had come rocketing back.

He spent half the night gritting his teeth, wallowing in self-pity.

Then along about 3:00 a.m. he mentally smacked himself. His injury was healing. He finally had some perspective on his mother's death. And for the first time in forever, he could imagine his long-term future.

That future included Sierra.

It had to.

He made up his mind to fight for her. And, by morning, his determination and excitement compensated for his lack of sleep.

Breakfast was always ready by six. Although he wanted to march straight to her room and make his case, he slowed himself down, ate a stack of pancakes and brought his brain cells to peak capacity with a cup of coffee.

He knew he couldn't come on too strong. If she wasn't feeling what he was feeling just yet, he had to respect that. What he needed here was time. He needed to buy himself enough time so she could see the potential for a life with him, a life for them together.

He rose from where he'd sat alone at the breakfast table and started a steady march past the kitchen, through the doors, to where the hallway narrowed into the staff quarters.

Her room was the second on the right.

The door was slightly ajar. That meant she was up, and he was glad to see that.

Not that he wouldn't have loved to find her in bed. The vision danced tantalizingly in his mind. But the sight would have been far too tempting and distracting. He'd have wanted to pull her into his arms like the last time they were together in that room.

"But you didn't say." McKinney's voice stopped him short outside the door.

What was his sister doing up this early? What was she doing with Sierra?

"No. I didn't. I wouldn't." Sierra's answer was adamant.

"But he was upset."

"He seemed upset." Sierra paused. "I mean, maybe I was reading it wrong. But he went from happy to—I don't know—really ticked off."

"You're sure he didn't figure it out?"

"When?" Sierra asked in a helpless tone. "It was too fast. One minute, he was talking about building himself a house, the next he was shouting at the boys that we were leaving."

"Okay." McKinney sounded relieved. "I mean, not okay. But okay. You know?"

"I know. If he ever found out about my real job." Sierra stopped talking.

"My brother is not a wellness coach kind of guy."

Dallas's confusion was turning to disquiet. What was going on here?

"We did the right thing," McKinney added.

"It feels like the wrong thing." There was a catch in Sierra's voice.

"You're not about to confess to him?" McKinney asked worriedly.

"No. Never. I won't."

Dallas pushed the door open in slow motion.

Both women looked his way, their eyes widening in alarm.

McKinney reacted first, coming to her feet, guilt written all over her face.

A dull roar pulsed in his ears, while his discovery made it hard to move his jaw. *"What,"* he ground out, asking Sierra first and foremost, "did you do?"

Twelve

Sierra was floored by the wounded expression in Dallas's eyes. They were dark, dull, bottomless with disappointment.

"I was worried about you." McKinney had the presence of mind to close the bedroom door behind him and give them some privacy.

"You're a wellness coach?" he demanded.

Sierra's throat went dry with regret.

"You were in a really bad way," McKinney said.

Dallas ignored his sister. "I want Sierra to tell me."

It was all Sierra could do to nod. She wanted to say something, wanted to explain, but she couldn't seem to form any words.

"That's what you do?" he asked. "You coach people who are what? Stressed, depressed, unable to cope?"

Sierra found her voice. "No. It's not like that."

"So, what's it like? Tell me. What did you think was so wrong with me that you had to *secretly* give me counseling?"

"There was nothing wrong with you."

"You were angry," McKinney put in. "You know it yourself, Dallas. You were angry with everything and everyone. I was afraid you'd desert the family."

"Living my own life isn't deserting anyone."

"You know what I mean," McKinney argued back. "And you can't say you weren't angry. You can't say you don't feel better."

"You've come so far," Sierra said.

"Are you sure?" he glared at her. "Because I'm plenty angry now."

She braced herself, knowing he had a right to that anger.

"What were you thinking?" he demanded. "How could you—" He seemed to stop himself from finishing the question.

"I shouldn't have slept with you," she said, firmly. "I know. I'm sorry."

His brow furrowed and he glanced at McKinney. "She knows? All that song and dance about keeping it private, and she *knows*?"

"I didn't know," McKinney quickly put. "I only just found out."

Dallas scoffed out a cold laugh. "I'm supposed to believe that?"

"This is my fault," Sierra said.

"Yes, it's your fault," he said. "You were never staying. You were never really here. How could you let me think—" He gave his head a rapid shake. "Never mind. It doesn't matter." He reached for the doorknob. "This family." His jaw hardened. "This family is never going to change."

"Dallas," McKinney pleaded.

But Dallas didn't pause. He was out the door, pulling it firmly shut behind him, leaving silence in his wake.

Sierra came to her feet. "Should I?"

"I don't know." McKinney sounded distraught. "I have no idea what we do."

"We can't just let him go." Sierra's instinct was to follow. But she didn't know what more she could say.

He knew the whole truth. There wasn't any further explanation that would exonerate her. What she'd done was wrong, and he had every right to be angry.

The best she could do was make it clear how sorry she was that he'd been hurt. She probably hadn't apologized profusely enough. She could at least do that.

She headed out the door and into the hallway for the family side of the mansion, passing the kitchen and entering the dining room.

Austin and Garrett both looked up from the table, clearly surprised that she'd interrupted their breakfast.

"I'm looking for Dallas," she said.

Austin canted his head toward the front door. "He just left."

She started that way. "Did he say where he was going?"

"Try the barn."

Sierra hoped he had gone to the barn rather than driving off in one of the trucks. She walked quickly, then trotted, then ran the few hundred yards to get to the main barn.

The big doors were open, and she hustled her way inside. Earthy scents filled her nostrils. Low voices were coming from the tack room. A horse whinnied in the distance. Farther in, horses shifted in their stalls, munching on their breakfast hay.

In a flash, she realized she was going to miss all this. She felt oddly at home here.

How had that happened so fast?

She went to the tack room but only found Rudy and Ethan.

"Have you seen Dallas?" she asked them, trying not to sound anxious.

They both shook their heads.

"Not today," Rudy said. "You need some help?"

"No, no. I'm fine. Just looking for Dallas." Her anxiety was ramping up as the minutes went by. Her stomach started to cramp, and her chest tightened.

She was afraid she wouldn't find him. She was also afraid she would.

She headed down the wide main aisle, past the wash bay and the supply cabinet, past empty stalls and the few with horses inside.

Cedric whinnied, but she didn't have time to stop and say hi.

She went the full length of the barn to the open door at the opposite end that led to a runout pen.

A movement caught in the corner of her eye, and she turned.

Dallas was at a corner stall, feeding an apple to the horse inside.

Their gazes met, and she slowed her steps.

"Hi," she said.

His shoulders stiffened, but he didn't answer.

She kept walking into the hardness of his gaze. "I'm sorry."

"So you said."

"I didn't mean for it to go this way."

"What way is that, Sierra?"

She chose her words carefully. "So far out of hand."

"You don't usually sleep with your clients?"

"Of course not." She took a beat and moderated her tone. "Never, ever before."

"None of my business if you do."

"It *is* your business. I want to explain—"

"You lied to me and slept with me, and you're sorry about it now. I get it. There really isn't anything more to explain." His tone was deceptively mild as he rubbed the nose of the horse in front of him. It nuzzled his shoulder in return.

"We were trying to help. McKinney was so worried. And I'm a licensed massage therapist."

The information didn't seem to sway him. "Should I have paid you?"

"That's not what I meant."

His mouth flattened in a thin line. "I get what you did. I get why you did it. It was wrong, but you didn't mean anything by it."

It would be easier if he'd shout at her. He should let it out and not let it fester inside.

"Is there anything I can do?" she asked pleadingly, daring to move a little closer. "Anything at all to make up for—"

"Breaking my heart?" he asked.

The words pierced her soul. "Dallas, I—"

"Didn't mean anything by it. You've made that perfectly clear. Could you leave, Sierra? Could you just leave?"

"I wanted to make it better." She felt desperate for him to understand.

"Well, you didn't." His look was cold and empty, like she'd disappeared.

He couldn't forgive her. He was right not to forgive her.

She didn't know how she'd ever forgive herself. "Please know McKinney had your best interests at heart."

"Sure." His tone was clipped. "So does Austin. So does my dad. And you know what? They're probably right. I should just listen to them, forget about thinking for myself, forget about following my instincts. If I'd only listened to all those brilliant people around me, the world would be a far, far better place."

"That's not what I meant."

"No? Should I listen to you, then? Should I take the advice of the massage therapist wellness guru? You must be very good. My family would never have hired you if you weren't very good."

"I was McKinney's friend. And you were hurting. And she was worried." Sierra knew she was repeating herself, but she didn't know what else to do. She couldn't walk away from him when he was like this. She'd come here to make things better for him, not to make them worse.

The horse whinnied and nodded its head. Another horse answered from deep in the barn. Then another and another.

She wondered if they felt the tension.

"I'll go," she said softly, realizing she wasn't helping at all.

"You do that."

She hesitated a moment longer, racking her brain for words of comfort. "You've come a long way, Dallas. It might not feel like it right now, but physically, emotionally, you've come a very long way."

His tone was emotionless, matching his expression. "Thank you so much for that expert opinion."

Heartsick, she turned to go.

"What am I missing?" Austin entered Dallas's bedroom, staring at the half-packed duffel bag laid out on the bed.

"Not a thing," Dallas answered as he methodically tossed in his shirts and jeans.

"You said you were going to think about it."

"I did think about it."

"And you decided to leave? Without telling anyone? Without giving us a chance to make you an offer?"

Dallas paused. "An offer?"

"Yes! To buy your land. Or lease your land. You're obviously selling out. If you were keeping it in the family, you'd have told us outright. You wouldn't be sneaking off in the night."

"I'm not sneaking off, and it's not night."

"It'll be night soon, and you didn't tell anyone you were leaving."

"McKinney knows."

"Bully for her. She doesn't know about the land. She doesn't know about Grampa's will."

"You can't afford to buy it." Dallas stated the obvious.

"So, you are going to sell."

Dallas gave a shrug. He hadn't decided what he was going to do, even though selling would mean he never had to worry about money ever again. Not that he ever worried about money. He didn't need much of it.

All he knew right now was that he had to leave. He couldn't risk seeing Sierra again. It was already impossible to cope with the memories pounding at his brain. He saw her everywhere he looked around here, and he feared he always would.

"Sierra was looking for you earlier."

"I know."

"You gave her riding lessons."

Dallas went back to packing, not seeing the relevance of the statement. "She wanted them."

"And the shoulder massages?"

"She's a trained professional."

"Good for her." Austin sounded impressed.

"Yeah," Dallas said shortly.

Austin moved to a chair and plopped down. "You fell for her."

Dallas didn't answer. He wasn't about to lie, but he sure didn't want to talk about his personal life with Austin.

"It didn't work out?" Austin prodded.

"You could say that."

"What did you do?"

"Me?" Dallas was incredulous.

"There had to be a reason why she left."

Something turned ice-cold inside Dallas.

Sierra had left?

"Were you a jerk?" Austin asked.

The ice-cold sensation turned to a disorienting sense of panic. "When did she leave?"

"Couple hours ago. You didn't know?" Austin peered at Dallas's expression. "Uh-oh."

Everything inside Dallas shouted at him to go after her. But he couldn't trust his own instincts. They kept getting him into trouble.

She didn't want him. She'd never wanted him. She was only here to do her job.

"You should see your face," Austin said.

Dallas gave himself a shake. He deliberately crossed to his closet and pulled another shirt from a hanger.

"Dude," Austin said in disgust.

Dallas spread the shirt on the bed and began to fold it.

"You're in love with her."

"Doesn't matter." There was no point in denying it. He'd look foolish trying.

"And you're going to let her go?"

"She didn't come here to fall for me. She came here to look after me. McKinney hired her to—I don't know— cheer me up or some stupid thing."

"Yeah? Probably a good idea. You were sure a pill for the rest of us."

"Ha, ha," Dallas answered sarcastically.

Austin seemed to consider for a moment. "What if she did anyway?"

"Did what?"

"Fell for you, bro. I take it that wasn't her plan. But the two of your seemed pretty close."

The sensation of Sierra washed over Dallas, all but staggering him in his path.

"I saw the way she looked at you," Austin said.

"Looked how?" Dallas's voice came out gruff with emotion. He knew he was grasping at straws, but he couldn't help himself.

Austin watched him closely. "Like she'd seen you naked and liked what she saw."

Dallas grasped the post of his bed.

"Aha!"

"You think?" Dallas was afraid to hope.

"The woman made love with you." Austin gestured to Dallas up and down. "You. That's not nothing. Because you're a bit rough around the edges, if you don't know. And she's beautiful and refined."

Dallas glared at his brother.

"Chill," Austin said. "It was an observation, that's all. I'm not your competition."

Austin was right.

Sierra had made love with Dallas—twice. She sure didn't need to do that to wellness coach him.

She'd laughed with him, challenged him. She'd been patient and steadfast and kind. Their friendship was more than professional, more than physical. He knew that right down to his bones.

A smile struggled to form on his lips.

"You don't go after her now, you'll regret it, brother," Austin said with conviction as a clap of thunder punctuated his words.

Sierra heard the boom of nearby thunder through the rain that clattered on the windshield of the pickup truck

McKinney had leant her for the drive into Granby. McKinney had tried to talk her into staying the night, but Sierra knew she couldn't do that. Every minute that passed, her heart broke a little further.

She needed to get off the ranch, away from Jagged Creek and out of Colorado. A clean break was her one and only hope. There were motels in Granby and a bus to Denver in the morning.

It seemed like an ironically perfect circle. The breakup with Roger had brought her onto the Hawkes ranch, and a breakup with Dallas was sending her off.

Not that it was a breakup with Dallas. They weren't even in a relationship.

Still, her monthslong engagement to Roger paled in comparison with the dalliance with Dallas. She didn't understand how that could be.

Lightning flashed as the evening turned to dark night. The mountains disappeared, and the trees were barely visible alongside the gravel road. She suddenly felt alone in a very big wilderness and wondered if she should have waited until morning.

She lifted her foot from the gas pedal and let the truck slow down. There was no hurry. Nothing waited for her in Granby except a lonely hotel room.

Her phone rang.

Watching the road out front, she reached inside her purse to find it.

It was a Colorado number, but not McKinney's.

Sierra's heart leaped for a moment at the thought that it might be Dallas. But just as quickly, she knew she didn't want to talk to him. There was nothing left to say.

She declined the call.

It rang a minute later, same number, and it occurred to her that something might be wrong. Something might even be wrong with McKinney. Otherwise, she'd be calling herself.

She accepted the call on speaker. "Hello?"

"Sierra?" It was Dallas.

She blew out a sigh. This was not the clean break she'd hoped. "Yes?"

"Where are you?"

"Driving."

"I know that. McKinney told me. But where?"

She looked out the windows at the blackness surrounding here. "I don't know."

"Will you come back?"

"No."

"Please come back."

"Why would I do that?" The last thing she needed was more recriminations. She'd cut the cord when she drove out the Hawkes ranch gates, and she had no intention of starting that process all over again. She was miles away now, and she intended to put many more miles between them.

"We should talk," he said.

"About what?" A touch of hysteria came into her voice.

"About us."

"There is no *us*."

"We made love, Sierra."

"It was an ill-advised fling that never should have happened." She started around a curve.

"Maybe."

"I'm glad you agree." Too late, she realized the curve was tighter than she'd expected.

"Still—"

"No!"

"What's wrong?"

Her front wheels hydroplaned on the slick road as she struggled with the line of the curve.

"Sierra?" he called out.

The back end of the truck broke loose, swinging off the edge of the road.

She let out a little shout as her body came tight against the seat belt. The truck clattered and bucked wildly beneath her, going over the hillside, crashing through some tree branches and bouncing off the trunks while the window shattered, and glass rained down behind her.

She jolted hard against the seat, and everything went still. The motor whined to silence, and the lights went out, while the rain blew through the shattered back window.

"Dallas?" she called out, feeling around for the phone.

She quickly stopped herself, afraid of cutting her hands on the broken glass.

The truck was on a steep angle. She didn't know how far she'd fallen down the bank. But at least it seemed stable for now. She gingerly felt her face, her torso and her limbs. She was wet in spots. She hoped it was rain and not blood.

Nothing hurt. But her adrenaline had to be pumping hard right now. She might not feel the pain for a few minutes.

She craned her neck, struggling to see something, anything. But it was pitch-dark under the storm clouds and deep in the trees.

Dallas would come, she told herself, checking for injuries once again, finding a stinging spot on her upper arm that felt stickier than rainwater. She gripped the spot tightly in case the bleeding was bad.

It might take a while, but he'd eventually find her.

The horrifying sound of the crash still echoed in Dallas's ears as he shouted instructions to his family and Newt, who was visiting the main house. Together, they mobilized every truck and four-wheeler on the ranch. They'd have taken horses too, but Sierra had left more than an hour ago. She had to be halfway to Jagged Creek.

While Dallas drove at breakneck speed, McKinney kept dialing Sierra's number.

"Nothing," she said after the tenth try.

"Her phone might be broken, or she's out of range."

He refused to consider Sierra was unconscious or worse. But this was a dangerous road at night, especially in the rain. They all knew that too well.

"Start here," McKinney said. "We're thirty miles out."

They'd divvied the road up into five-mile sections, with Dallas taking the farthest from the ranch. He didn't trust anyone else to drive fast enough.

He slowed to a crawl. McKinney shined a floodlight, sweeping both sides of the road.

"We'll find her," McKinney said.

"I know." He needed it to be soon. He needed to hold her in his arms and reassure himself she was alright. She *had* to be alright.

"You doing okay?" McKinney asked.

"I'm fine," he said tersely. His mental state was the last thing they needed to worry about right now.

"It has to remind you of Mom."

"It reminds everyone of Mom. But this is different."

"I agree."

"Good. Can we stop talking about it?"

"Sure. So long as you're okay."

A flash of metal in the floodlight beam caught his eye. "What's that? Down there." He stabbed his index finger in the right direction as he came to a stop. "Shine the light."

"I'm shining. I'm shining."

They both peered into the night.

"It's the truck!" he all but shouted, clamping down on the emergency brake and shifting the truck into Park.

He put on a headlamp and slung a coiled rope and first aid pack over his shoulder. "Call everybody."

"I am. Should you go down there alone?"

"I'm sure not waiting up here." He exited into the driving rain.

"It's steep," McKinney called from behind him.

"I'll be fine. Keep the light shining down there."

"I'll follow you."

"No. Don't. Wait until I see what I need."

"Alright." She hit the hazard lights, then followed him outside, pointing the beam of her floodlight on the mangled truck.

"Sierra?" Dallas called and then listened.

Nothing.

"Dad?" McKinney said into the phone. "We found her. We're just past the thirty-mile mark." She paused. "We don't know yet. Dallas is headed down the bank."

McKinney's voice faded behind him as Dallas scrambled from tree-hold to tree-hold on the slippery slope.

"Sierra?" he called out again. "I'm coming."

She didn't answer, and it took painful minutes for him to get to the truck, agonizing seconds longer to make his way along to the driver's side.

He opened the door. "Sierra?" he asked softly.

Her eyes fluttered open in the beam of his headlamp, and she smiled. "About time."

"Are you hurt?"

"Not much. A little, maybe. My arm."

He looked at her arm, the light revealing a deep gash that was still oozing blood. "That's more than not much."

He extracted some gauze from the first aid pack, talking as he wrapped her arm. "Anything else hurt? Did you lose consciousness?"

"I didn't pass out," she said. "I got a little woozy and cold after a while."

"Good. That's good. Not the woozy part. The not-passing-out part."

She managed another smile as he finished wrapping her arm.

"Can you walk?"

She nodded. "Sure. Yeah. Get me out of here."

Thirteen

Sierra awoke in the ranch's guest room where she'd slept the first night. She blinked at the beamed ceiling and the glass-paned light fixture above the bed.

Pain flared in her upper arm, and she remembered the night before.

"How are you feeling?" Dallas's voice startled her. He rose from an armchair, moved to her bedside and took her hand.

"Okay." She coughed a little over the word, her throat feeling scratchy dry.

"They gave you ten stitches," he said.

"I remember." The pain medication had left her groggy, but she recalled driving back to the ranch, Dallas carrying her into this room, McKinney helping her into bed. "Thanks for that."

"Seriously? Thanks?"

"You rescued me."

"I'm the reason you needed rescuing in the first place."

She was baffled by the statement. "How do you figure that?"

He gave her hand a squeeze. "I chased you away."

"I left."

He sat down on the edge of the bed. "I'm sorry we fought."

She shook her head. "You had every right to be angry."

The more she thought about it, the more she regretted not being up front with him from the start. She'd tried to gain his trust while building on a lie. She should have known better.

He raised her hand to his lips and gently kissed the back of her knuckles. "I don't want to argue with you."

"Good." She closed her eyes and breathed a sigh. Her arm stung with the stitches, and the rest of her hurt too. It felt like every muscle and joint had been stretched to the breaking point.

He smoothed her hair back from her forehead. "You want to sleep some more?"

"What time is it?"

"A little after noon."

The information jolted her. "Seriously?" She tried to sit up.

"Whoa. Stay put. You need to rest."

She sat up anyway.

He pulled a mock frown. "You're not going to take my advice, are you?"

"I feel okay." She did. She was sore, but she was fine. Thanks to Dallas. She put her hand on his forearm. "Seriously. Thank you."

He swallowed. "It was Austin, really."

"It was you." She remembered that part very clearly, the relief she'd felt when she heard his voice, saw the beam of light, felt him grasp her tight.

"He told me to go after you. That's why I called first."
Dallas gave an ironic little smile. "Austin always gives the
best advice."

She'd never heard Dallas talk about his brother like that.
To the contrary, he mostly seemed annoyed by Austin and
his insistence Dallas should quit the rodeo, not to mention
his ideas for modernizing the ranch. The two brothers
rarely seemed to see eye to eye on anything.

"He told me to go after my mother that night," Dallas said, a faraway look coming into his eyes. "I waited. I
should have gone sooner."

Sierra chose her words carefully. "You can't know that
it would have helped."

He gave the barest of nods. "I think I finally figured that
out. For years I was sure I could have saved her. But we'll
never know. I just have to accept that and move forward."

Sierra stroked her hand along his arm. "There are a
thousand things in life like that—split-second decisions,
missed traffic lights, going left instead of right, missing
an opportunity to say or do something that might have
changed everything. Second-guessing is a road to no-
where."

Dallas nodded.

"You called me last night," she said. "Luckily for me."

"Luckily for me," he said with a gentle smile. "Austin
thinks I should marry you."

Sierra gave her head a little shake, certain she couldn't
have heard right. Maybe the pain pills were still messing
with her mind. "What?"

"He's pretty adamant. And, I have to say, I'm inclined
to take his advice given his track record."

"Is that a joke?" Sierra scrambled to make sense of the
conversation.

"Not really. He can see how incredibly good you are for me. Plus, he noticed I was in love with you, so—" Dallas gave a shrug.

Sierra's chest bloomed with astonishment and happiness.

Dallas loved her? He *loved* her? Was that truly what he was saying?

He leaned in. "I love you, Sierra," he whispered as his lips touched hers.

She wrapped her arms around him, forgetting her pain, forgetting everything but the strength and security of his arms.

"I love you," she whispered.

"Thank goodness for that." He drew back, his eyes alight with a wide smile.

"So, are you proposing?" She really wasn't clear on what was happening here.

He shook his head.

She squelched a flash of disappointment. It was enough that he loved her. That was everything.

"There's something I have to do first," he said. Then he gave a teasing grin. "But, when I do ask, will you say yes?"

She cocked her head. "I'm not sure you get to know the answer in advance."

"Why not?" he asked with exaggerated bafflement. "You know you will. Austin's never wrong."

She framed his face with her hands. "Is this really about Austin?"

"Hey, I've learned my lesson."

"I'm not sure you have." She deepened her voice and intoned: "Marry me, sweetheart, because my brother wants you to."

"Not the most romantic proposal in the world?"

"Not even close."

He gave her a quick kiss. "Good thing this isn't a proposal, then. I'll come up with something better."

"You should do that," she said, nodding while she stifled a laugh.

Dallas's grandmother's ring box felt clunky in his pocket.

Years ago, he'd made a pact with his two brothers. Whoever proposed first got their choice of the three rings: their mother's, grandmother's and great-grandmother's. All were pretty in their own way, but his grandmother's ring with its round diamond bracketed by square-cut sapphires matched the sparkle in Sierra's eyes.

It was unique, like she was. It was the perfect choice.

He'd been impatient for the past couple of days to make it official. But he'd wanted to give her some time to heal. He didn't want the memories of his proposal to be dulled by painkillers, or worse, marred by pain. He wanted the experience to be nothing but joyful.

"Is this it?" she asked now as they crossed the footbridge over the burbling creek on the back patio. "Is it happening now?"

It wasn't the first time she'd teasingly asked him that. In fact, it had become a running joke between them.

"No," he answered. Then he made a show of looking around. "But this would be a great spot."

"No kidding. It's beautiful out here."

"But I might want to wait for the sunset," he said.

"Two more hours? You're going to make me wait two more hours?"

He tugged her close and dropped a kiss at her temple. "Who says it's going to be today?"

"What if I proposed to you?"

"Don't do that."

"Why? Would you say no?"

"Not a chance. But you'll ruin the surprise."

"News flash. It's not exactly a surprise anymore."

"I wouldn't be so sure about that. Oh, look." Dallas nodded through the windows to the dining room. "Victor said he was making Chicago pizza for dinner."

"Yum." She grinned and picked up the pace. "My favorite."

"Really?" he asked with mock surprise, since everyone knew it was her favorite. "You like pizza?"

"You think he made milkshakes, too?" Sierra had declared vanilla milkshakes topped with swirls of whipped cream the perfect accompaniment to Victor's pizza. "Let's go," she said enthusiastically, tugging him along.

They entered through the French doors to find McKinney, Austin and his father taking their seats at the table that held two giant pizza pies.

Victor was passing out vanilla milkshakes, as Dallas had known he would.

Their father sat at the head of the table, while Dallas pulled out a chair for Sierra.

She gave him a happy grin over her shoulder as she sat down across from McKinney.

"Can you bring us some champagne?" Dallas asked Victor. "The Crystal Gold." He glanced to his father. "If Dad doesn't mind."

"What's the occasion?" his father asked.

Dallas withdrew the sky-blue velveteen ring box from his pocket and flipped it open. "I'm asking Sierra to marry me."

McKinney squealed in delight.

"Victor," his father called out heartily. "Champagne all around."

"She hasn't said yes yet," Austin pointed out.

"She'll say yes," Dallas said, smiling into Sierra's eyes.

"You got me," she said. "You distracted me with vanilla milkshakes, and you got me." She looked down at the ring, and her eyes widened. "Oh, my."

"It was my grandmother's," he said.

"It's stunning."

"Nice choice," his father said approvingly.

"Finally," Austin said, rising from his chair. "The man takes my advice."

"Oh, me first," McKinney said, hopping up faster than Austin and rushing around the table to Sierra.

"I should get the ring on her finger," Dallas told his sister.

Victor returned and loudly popped the champagne cork.

Sierra held out her hand. "Yes," she said as Dallas extracted the ring. "In case I wasn't clear yet. Absolutely yes."

The ring slid on like it was made for her, and Dallas kissed her deeply.

"Let me see," McKinney lifted Sierra's hand.

His father poured the champagne.

"Welcome to the family," Austin said, giving Sierra a quick hug.

"I heard it was your idea."

"All the best ideas are mine," Austin said.

"I'm starting a rodeo stock operation," Dallas said, giving Austin an arched look. "Up at White Foam Falls. Not all the good ideas are yours."

"That's fantastic, son," his father said, looking both moved and delighted.

"Okay by you?" Dallas asked Sierra.

"We're building the house?"

He nodded. "We're building the house. Having some kids too if that's what you want too."

She flung her arms around his neck and squeezed him

tight, whispering in his ear. "It's exactly what I want. I love you so much, Dallas."

"A toast," his father said, passing around the glasses of champagne.

"I love you more," Dallas whispered with a final squeeze before letting her go.

"To family," his father said, raising his glass. "To my new daughter and the bright future of the Hawkes."

* * * * *

For more charming romances from acclaimed author Barbara Dunlop and Harlequin Desire, visit www.Harlequin.com today!

HARLEQUIN
PLUS

Try the best multimedia subscription service for romance readers like you!

Read, Watch and Play.

Experience the easiest way to get the romance content you crave.

Start your **FREE TRIAL** at
<u>www.harlequinplus.com/freetrial</u>.